THE RED THREAD
OF DESTINY

THE RED THREAD OF DESTINY

M.C. Bradley

LEON SMITH

PUBLISHING

To the brokenhearted. To the lonely. To you.

Contents

Prologue

There is an ancient legend that spans across the Asian continent about a certain red thread that binds two lovers together by true love. The Red Thread of Destiny cannot be affected by its possessor no matter the circumstance, time, or place. The thread will endure through it all. No matter how much the thread stretches or tangles, it will remain unscathed.

Some believers in the Red Thread of Destiny also state if the love is true, the lovers can feel their pinkies tighten or see a shimmer of red twine twinkle when they hold hands. Otherwise, the thread remains unseen. Some legends posit you can trip over this thread. If lovers seemingly fall over nothing, this is why. Believers also say that when these things begin to happen, the pair are growing nearer to each other.

Now, the presence of the Red Thread of Destiny doesn't always mean that those two who are entwined with one another are destined to love each other, but they will meet. It's hard to determine the meaning of the thread at times, but that's the fun part. A person can have more than one thread tied to their pinkie.

Now, I invite you to enter a story—maybe not much of a legend—of a woman discovering the Red Thread of Destiny to find her true love. We begin with a woman, Crystal Ann Alston.

Chapter One

"Crystal Ann," sung a friendly voice, bringing me back to the real world. A figure to my right sat at the corner of my desk.

A small grin crossed my face as I realized it was Jess. I sighed as I looked up from my computer with an eyebrow raised, expecting the worst. "Oh, Jess, is there something you need?" I asked.

Jess is probably the only actual friend I have in this place full of gossip and news. Every day, so much of the news gets mixed up with the gossip that runs through the offices.

"Well, me being a techy, and you being a reporter who can leave and doesn't have to deal with, well, technical things . . . could you please get us some coffee from Starbucks?" Jess asked with a little pout.

I scoffed as I leaned back in my chair, as if thinking about her proposition. "All right. It shouldn't be too much trouble. What do you want?"

"Black with cream, the usual, and only way to have coffee," Jess said as she brought out a few dollars from her small pocket. "Get me what you can with this, please. I am on the tight end of things this month."

"As you wish, Jess." I leaned forward, taking her money. I jumped out of my chair with enthusiasm. "I will be back as soon as I can. Starbucks lines are *always* a hassle. *Especially* in New York City."

"Oh, you and I both know you can count on that," she laughed. Jess walked back to her area solemnly, as if seeing my enthusiasm about leaving was rubbing it in her face—that I could leave and she couldn't. I noticed as Jess had returned to her station, she was immediately greeted with more work by her fellow technicians.

I grabbed my wallet before leaving. While I walked away, the cell phone on my desk suddenly buzzed. I shrugged it off, leaving it and continuing to the elevator to the street.

I pushed open the doors and smog filled my lungs as I took in a deep breath of the *fresh air* that is slowly killing everyone. Everyone knows it; this pollution is killing us, but we choose to ignore it at the same time.

I scanned up and down the street and walked to the nearest Starbucks sitting on the corner. When I peered at the darkened windows, I noticed it was closed. I sighed and growled to myself about it not being open. The inconvenience was killer. I stopped and peeked in to see why it wasn't open. It looked like it had been closed for a movie set. People were walking around, working, unlike me. Several lights and wires were spread across the floor.

"How do they even work without tripping all over the place?" I wondered aloud as I gawked at the makeshift studio.

"Excuse us," a redheaded chick snarled. As I looked back and up at her, I saw she was with a tall, handsome, blond man who was walking behind her.

"Sorry," I whispered sheepishly. I stood up straight, trying to hold my ground but moved out of their way. Her aura overpowered mine.

The blond man's eyes met mine. I blushed, knowing he was the movie star, Cole Dakota. We kept our eyes on each other until he entered the closed Starbucks with the redheaded woman.

I placed my hands over my cheeks for a brief moment before turning away, trying to calm myself down. *He is one of the best actors in Hollywood, arguably of course. I may just be a little biased.*

"Well," I said to myself, clearing my throat. I straightened my shirt to help shield me better against the autumn wind, "at least Starbucks are on every block." I tried to get my mind off Wonder boy and set my mind on my mission.

I began to walk, but stopped, still entranced. I couldn't get him out of my head. I glanced back, looking through the dark glass into the Starbucks. To my surprise, I found Cole

Dakota staring back at me. I gasped and turned away. I strolled away, embarrassed.

I kept going until I found another Starbucks a couple of blocks down the street. I sighed and shook my head with disappointment when I saw a long line in front of me.

My mind wondered as I stood in line. I did my best not to think of Cole. *It was amazing seeing him with my own two eyes. Focus, Crystal Ann!*

"Next!" I heard loudly. My train of thought disappeared. I looked up to see that I was not the next in line. There was still a long way to go.

After waiting for what seemed like forever, a man approached too close to where I was, in the front of the line. "Hey, I am in a hurry. Please, let me cut," begged the man to the person in front of me.

"We're all in a hurry here, dude. Just get in the back," the man said with a deep Brooklyn accent.

"You can cut in front of me. I don't mind," I said as I stepped back, letting him into the line.

Many people behind me sighed and moaned. I felt their eyes rolling at my decision. *I was close to the front too, but, helping people could give me some good karma. I think I need it. I believe if we are all kind to each other, the world would be a better place. It's completely understandable, though, that most people are selfish. Nobody's perfect.*

After a couple more minutes of waiting, I finally made it to the counter, but to my surprise, I was greeted with an unhappy employee, a teenager who hated his job. He wasn't much of a looker either, which may have contributed to his poor attitude. The boy had an oily mop under his hair net and acne spread across his face.

I asked as politely as possible for Jess' coffee with cream and iced tea for me. I was hoping to make his day at least a little better by being nice.

I paid cash, as to not hold up the rest of the line. I also stepped to the side and realized that maybe it would've been a good idea to have brought my phone. I could've fiddled with it while I waited.

A few minutes later, I got my beverages. I hurried out to the street and back toward work, hoping I hadn't been gone too long. I thought people might notice I was missing. *I shouldn't have spent so much time gawking at Cole Dakota.*

I walked down the street back toward the office. I began to saunter past the Starbucks where the set was. My heart wanted to see Cole Dakota just one more time, when, suddenly, the door flew open right in front of me. I stepped back. I saw my reflection in the glass with wide eyes. My heart skipped a beat before it raced, full of adrenaline, and my eyes wandered down to the drinks with caution. I sighed, relieved. I had almost spilled something very hot or really cold on myself.

"Rachel, please!" Cole said as he walked out.

"Cole, be careful! You almost hit that person," the redheaded woman, whom I assume was Rachel, scolded as Cole's and my eyes met again for another moment.

"Sorry." He apologized a little impatiently, but I could tell that his frustration wasn't directed at me.

I looked away from him shyly and reached to sip some of my iced tea when a man bumped right into me from behind. My right arm jolted to the side then toward me, causing my iced tea to splash all over me. I gasped as quietly as I could when the ice-cold beverage hit my chest.

Afraid to see the damage that had been done, I looked down. My favorite shirt was soaked with tea. It dripped down my once-clean blouse. A fresh breeze swept through, chilling me. I sucked in a deep breath, holding in my slight cry from the wind that caused this accident to be so much worse. I shivered slightly, trying to hold in my discomfort. I looked up at the two people in front of me, and they stared back.

"Excuse me," I coughed and tried to walk around them.

"Do you want a new shirt or something?" asked Cole, stopping me with his offer.

I blinked a few times, trying to register what was just said to me. Was it said to *me?*

No one else got in an accident with their clothing, at least none that I saw in front of me. It's gotta be me. He's really talking to me.

In awe, I stayed silent, feeling sheepish, as I slowly turned my head around. "It's—it's really nothing," I said, trying to brush it off.

"She's right, Cole; she's got better things to do," said the redhead, as if she really wanted to rip him one.

I puffed out some breath and turned away to leave when he gently touched my arm, ignoring the redheaded lady and beckoning me to look at him.

"Please, it'll be my pleasure," he said quietly. "I'll even replace that drink you had," he offered in a sweet tone. He had a polite smile on his face, making me feel welcome.

"Cole!" exclaimed the woman impatiently.

"Um, sure . . . Why not?" I said after eyeing the woman for a moment. She didn't seem too keen about me staying, but I was freezing. I looked at her again and something about her attitude made me ask Cole, without thinking, if he had something warmer for me to wear.

He grinned with a nod, causing the redhead to snort with disappointment.

Her eyes narrowed. "Cole, you're a piece of work." She turned away and stormed back inside.

"Phew," Cole breathed out, relieved. "You saved me from her wrath."

I couldn't help smirking. However, I composed myself and made the smirk disappear as quickly as it came. "I thought you could save yourself, Charming," I said, a little flirty.

Cole cracked half a smile as he chuckled. "You're a sassy one. I like that."

"You only like it because I'm cute."

Cole stopped himself from smiling wider as he shook his head. "Let's get you that shirt I promised," he said, putting his arm around my shoulders and leading me inside.

I raised my eyebrows and blushed. *He's a gentleman. It's really nice to know he's really kind and it's not a facade.*

We walked in, and the red-headed lady brought me the shirt that I was promised.

"Thanks," I said, as nicely as I could to both Cole and Rachel. I stepped away from Cole as he wandered off.

"Here, let me hold that for you," Rachel said, taking the drink. "What kind of drink is this?"

"Black with cream."

"I'll replace this, too, so it's not cold when you come back out," she offered, as if trying to make up for her behavior. "What were you drinking?"

I was surprised. "Thank you. That's very kind of you. Oh, and the drink was iced tea." She gave a curt nod and walked toward the counter for the drinks.

I walked into the bathroom and into the biggest stall. I slipped off my shirt. I sighed a breath of relief at removing the cold, wet shirt. I took some toilet paper and dabbed myself to make sure I was as dry as possible.

Too bad my bra got wet too, I thought to myself, putting the other shirt on as delicately as I could so my bra didn't soak through the dry shirt. *It's definitely not work-appropriate, but my boss will just need to deal.*

I made my way out, holding my dirty shirt in my left hand and looking in the mirror as I walked out of the bathroom. My hair was a bit of a mess because of the wind. *I really hate having these frayed ends. They're not fun at all. Maybe I should cut my hair short.*

As I walked out, I noticed something to my left. I jumped back as Cole was waiting there for me with my drinks.

"Oh, sorry," Cole laughed. "Didn't mean to startle you."

"It's fine," I said as I put my dirty shirt over my arm and reached for the drinks, but he pulled them back, as if teasing me.

"If you want your drinks, you're going to need to agree to have a date with me," he said.

I smiled as big as I could. "A date?"

"Yes! A date. But, before you agree, I'd like to ask you for your name," he said as he leaned toward me.

I scooted back as if afraid more drink would spill on me. He quickly backed off when he noticed that I was a bit uncomfortable.

"Interesting. A movie star asking a regular girl out on a date. Won't I take advantage of you and your money?" I asked, as if I were every other fan girl who was stalking him, holding to the dream of dating or marrying him for his money and good looks.

"Well, since you brought that up, I now know that money isn't your motive."

"How sly, Mr. Dakota," I said, grinning.

He laughed. "You are a very smooth talker. . . my friend."

"Oh? Now we're friends? That is very interesting," I said. "You don't even know my name."

"Well, I would know it if you would tell me."

"Oh, there's no need for that," I said.

"Cole, you're on soon," Rachel called to him. She seemed calmer than before.

"I guess I'll remain the biggest mystery of your life. Won't you escort me to the door?" I turned to walk out without my drinks.

He quickly followed me. "I haven't met a girl quite like you before. You haven't asked for an autograph yet or anything. It's a little surprising." He spoke in a sober voice.

I stopped and turned toward him, our eyes meeting for several moments. I felt goosebumps as we looked at one another. His face was serious, almost sad. I had no idea what he could be sad about.

"Well," I managed to say as I looked away, "I know that you are a human like me. No matter how much richer you are compared to me, we'll both be buried in the same ground. I see you as my equal, not some god like other girls—or people, I mean—do."

His eyes twinkled for a moment. I had spoken to him truthfully and casually, as if we really were friends. It was probably something he wasn't used to. *The girls he's met probably treat him like he's some glorious being or something.* A half smile came to his face as he looked at me and pondered my answer.

I started to apologize because he was quiet, and I thought I had hurt his feelings in some way. He spoke first, "I was going to exchange these drinks for your name and number, to get that date later, but, I think these drinks would trade well for what you just told me. Humbling me. And, of course, you'll be the biggest mystery to me."

I was shocked as he handed me the iced tea and coffee. I took it graciously but didn't say anything as I sipped at my drink.

"Thanks," I said as I looked at the floor. It was spotless like everything in a movie would be.

"You're welcome. Where are you headed to?" he asked.

My attention was drawn back to his face when he asked this question. I grinned as I told him I was heading back to work.

"How far?" he asked.

"Just down the block," I sighed. "I should be getting back now."

"Would you mind if I walked you?" he asked.

I didn't even think about what I said as my mouth moved on its own. "I'd like you to. It's fun talking to you, but you have a job of your own. You were just called." I cleared my throat after I spoke, surprised by my own words.

He chuckled as he shook his hand in front of his face. "Let me walk you back to work. There'll be a lunch break soon anyway. I can postpone the shoot if I am hungry enough." He grinned with a small wink. He seemed to shrug off staying near the set as we walked toward the door.

"I should be fine by myself," I said, trying not to cause more trouble between him and the redheaded woman.

"Are you sure? It'd be my pleasure to escort you back," he said, almost begging to be taken away from work.

"Cole!" said his redheaded friend. "Where do you think you're going? I called you just now!"

"As I thought," I said, with a nod for him to go. "No need to walk me to my job. I'll be fine. I do live in New York City after all. I know how to take care of myself."

"But, Rachel . . . " Cole started, as he turned around to the woman.

"No, Cole. Sorry, ma'am, but you'll have to stop distracting my star and leave," she stated coldly.

I cleared my throat once again as my nose twitched. *She really has a fiery soul.* "Fine," I said. "It was a pleasure, Cole Dakota, to meet you. I'll see you on the silver screen."

Before I could be stopped by him again, I left thinking: *He sure was put in his place by Rachel, the redheaded hothead.*

Chapter Two

I heard loud footsteps. "Alston!" Mr. Ulysses, my boss, shouted to me.

I turned around to see his face almost in mine. I backed away as I scanned his face to see how he was feeling toward me.

"Yes, Boss?" I asked.

"You should know full well this isn't a gossip magazine. It's a newspaper," he said.

"I am aware."

He scoffed. "Then what is this article about Cole Dakota that you want put into my newspaper?"

"It isn't gossip. It is news. I am telling the girls and whoever else of New York their idol is in town. Although they might have already known. I am sure we will sell a few more newspapers with my article about Cole Dakota inside of it. It's not gossip—just news of his arrival."

"How did you know he arrived?" my boss asked. Pushing for answers, he slammed the newspaper down onto my desk like a true reporter.

I grinned. "A credible source—myself."

Mr. Ulysses sighed and put his hand over his eyes. "Well, as I said, this isn't a gossip magazine. I didn't put it into this morning's newspaper. But, could you do an article about a life's day as a celebrity? Instead of just saying that this superstar is here in New York? That's what a gossip magazine would do." He calmed down as he spoke.

My excitement grew as a big story finally crossed my path. "If I can find him, Boss, I'll definitely do this story for you."

"Well, Alston, let's hope you do find him." He turned back to his office.

I let out a deep breath as I leaned back in my chair. I watched Jess walk over with a stunned look on her face.

"What did he say?" she asked softly. She moved the newspaper out of the way and sat down at the corner of my desk.

"He gave me an article idea that he wants me to do. I need to find Cole Dakota. But I am almost certain they moved out of the place I last saw him."

"Can't help with that," she said.

"I know." I checked my watch. "I am going to go get lunch." I stood up, putting my phone and wallet into my pocket. "I'll see you later, Jess."

Jess nodded as she went back to her station.

I made my way out of the building with a heavy heart. *I am going to have to find Cole in this big city. He might not even be here in New York anymore.*

I began walking down the street toward the Starbucks they had used for filming. It looked as if it was back to normal operation. I stared into the busy coffee cafe as someone stopped beside me. I saw a blurry reflection through the glass.

"Missing someone?" he asked.

"No. I am just overwhelmed by a job that I was given. I have to find someone that I don't think is here anymore," I said.

"What's his name?" the man asked.

"You know, you're getting on my nerves, Mister, because I don't think it's really any of your concern," I growled. I turned toward the man and scanned him up and down. I saw a blond man with big sunglasses covering his eyes and a baseball cap on his head.

"Would his name be Cole Dakota?" he asked with a grin.

"Have you been following me around?" I turned toward him, crossed my arms, and popped my hip out to the side.

"Not entirely. A star is busy, ya know," he said a little softer, continuing to look through the window.

"It's called stalking."

"It's called letting someone escort you back to work. I can't help but chase a brunette with sparkling honey eyes," he said.

I felt the blood rush to my cheeks as I stared into his piercing blue eyes, searching for the lie. It wasn't there. I looked away for a moment. "You still stalked me."

"I thought you'd be flattered. I find you interesting, Crystal Ann," he said.

I tried to hide that I was a bit nervous because he knew my name. "Well, if you know my name, then it's 'Miss Alston' to you."

"Well, Miss Alston," Cole said, "Would you mind going on that date with me?"

"I assume you've already had a P.I. check me out," I asked. I changed the subject, wanting to know how he knew my name.

"I can't deny I wanted to see if you had a clean past and to actually see who you were before trying to approach you again. Didn't want to freak you out too much," he said.

"It's a bit too late for that." I was a bit disappointed by his words. "You could've asked?"

"You didn't seem to want to talk." he countered. "You also weren't giving me anything to go on."

"Where would dinner be?" I asked. I was caving to his wants.

"Wherever you want," he said, leaning toward me.

"Surprise me." I said. "I don't like Indian food, so keep that in mind."

"Why are you suddenly so keen on going on a date with me now, huh?" Cole asked. A smile crossed his face.

I told him the truth. "Well, my boss wants a piece on what it is to be a celebrity for a day."

"For your newspaper?"

"Of course," I said with a nod. "What else would it be for? It would be a nice piece to add in for a special edition of my newspaper."

"Could I talk to your boss, then?"

"You could do what you want without my permission." I shrugged.

"Including following you around?" Cole tipped his hat.

I rolled my eyes playfully. "You got me there."

"So you won't press charges?" he asked.

"Fine. You got me to give you permission to do so, I guess. It's weird because *you* are the celebrity. I should be stalking you."

"So, you would stalk me then?" he asked as he peered over his sunglasses.

"No, I wouldn't. You deserve your privacy," I said quickly, not wanting to talk about it further.

"Interesting." He appeared deep in thought.

"I still need to interview you," I said.

"One day in the life of a celebrity?"

"Yes," I nodded.

"I still want to talk to your boss first," he said.

"Why?" I was curious.

"I won't get your hopes up." He winked.

"Seems interesting enough, I guess. Let's go." I walked around him, ignoring my craving for lunch as I guided us back toward my office building.

Cole Dakota, the celebrity, followed behind me. I never thought I'd meet a superstar in my life, let alone one interested in me.

Chapter Three

I leaned back in my chair, staring into Mr. Ulysses' office. He and Cole Dakota were having a nice conversation from what I could see. They were laughing and smiling as their dialogue went on.

"Wow, the famous Cole Dakota," Jess said as she came over and sat on my desk next to me. "You really did meet him then, huh? Just wow."

"Did the wildfire spread that fast?" I asked, looking around at everyone. They were all trying not to stare at Cole Dakota through the glass.

"Yeah. Especially when everyone saw you walk in with him. His arm over your shoulders." She winked and nudged me with her arm. I gave her a small shake of my head.

I tried not to smile. "That didn't happen. We just walked in, and I introduced him to our boss."

"Do you know what they're talking about?" she asked, changing the subject.

"I have no idea. Probably the article that Mr. Ulysses wants me to do. I guess we'll see. The boss is calling me in." He pointed right at me and signaled for me to come in. I stood up. I felt everyone's eyes turn to me.

"Good luck," she teased.

"Thanks."

I slowly opened the door. "Yes, sir?" I asked.

"Close the door, Alston," he said. "Come sit down."

I closed the door behind me and sat down next to *Cole Dakota*.

He began, "Mr. Dakota . . . "

"Oh, just Cole," he insisted.

Mr. Ulysses smiled at Cole's modesty and continued. "Cole loves the idea of my segment. But he doesn't think just a day in his life is sufficient enough. He said he wants the section of his life to be two weeks. To make sure we get enough information. I want this article to be extra special."

"Two weeks?" I questioned. "Are you sure, Sir?"

"Yes, you will follow him everywhere. Wherever he goes, you go. His agent agreed. She wants to get him more publicity with this article, so it better be good or you're fired."

"What if I do not wish to take this job?" I asked.

My boss raised an eyebrow at the question and looked toward Cole.

Cole spoke first. "I think I want you for the job. I don't know what your boss will do to you if you say no to him, but I know if you say yes, you'll have more fun with me than sitting at your desk." Cole winked and chuckled.

I raised my eyebrows and couldn't help but grin. "Sir?"

"He chose you himself as well. I think you would be good for the job, Alston."

"I won't give you the story unless it's her with me," Cole said.

"Alston," Mr. Ulysses said in a stern voice. I could see his heart racing at the thought of a good story slipping through the cracks. "Do you want to miss a big article like this? Not everyone can say that they spent two weeks with Cole Dakota."

I sighed. "As long as I get good money for this."

My boss rolled his eyes and cleared his throat. "Get to work, Alston."

"When do I start then?" I asked.

"Tomorrow."

"What about an earlier start?" Cole asked.

I stood up and looked down at Cole who was looking at Mr. Ulysses seriously.

He sighed once again. "Are you sure, Mr.—I mean, Cole?"

"I don't think an extra day would hurt." He shrugged casually.

I crossed my arms. I looked toward Jess who was staring intently at me from my desk. I shook my head at her slightly. This was an unbelievable situation to me, almost like a ridiculous dream.

"Then, Alston, you start today," Mr. Ulysses said. "Follow him around wherever he goes."

"I like the sound of that," Cole whispered to himself.

I crossed my arms over my chest, trying to act professional. "What are my hours of pay then, Boss?"

"Excuse us, Cole," Mr. Ulysses said, "I need to talk to Miss Alston alone for a moment."

"Of course." He walked out the door and closed it behind him. Out of the corner of my eye, I saw people slowly flocking to him.

"Do you want to get fired? Pressing for money?" he hissed, "In front of a guest no less!" He stood up from his desk, his face red from his blood pressure rising at my audacity.

"If that'll move me up in the world, Boss. He favors me, so you won't get your story if you fire me or even try to take me off the article," I said as I straightened myself. I raised my chin even though I felt as if I was about to wet my pants. "I want to know how I am going to be paid and how much. I want to make sure I am taken care of, after all."

"What do you want, then?" he asked.

"Just double my pay for the next two weeks, then after that you can put my pay back," I said. I held my breath, hoping it would calm my heart.

"Double?!" he hissed. He rose from his chair, slamming his hands on his desk.

"For the trouble of having to follow him around and the paparazzi. As I said, I want to make sure I am taken care of after all of this is over," I stated.

"Fine. It's just for two weeks," Mr. Ulysses said, as he loosened his tie. He took a handkerchief from his pocked and dabbed the sweat from his forehead as he gritted his teeth.

"It starts today, doesn't it?"

He let out a mean growl. "Of course it does."

"Shall I send him back in?"

"No, since your pay starts today. . . Go!" He shooed me away, as he pushed back his graying comb-over. "Get back to work!" he shouted through the open door.

Everyone reluctantly walked back to their desks.

"He looked a little mad at what you had to say," Cole commented as I walked out.

"He's never happy when someone forces money from his pocket," I said.

As I walked toward my desk, Jess put a hand on my shoulder. "So, do you have the article then?"

"I did get it," I said with a nod, trying to hold back my smile. "I'm getting double pay for two weeks!" I whispered to her, still trying to contain my excitement. "I've got to get right on it though." I rummaged through my desk, grabbing my phone, notepad, and pen, and stuffing them into my pockets. "I'll see you later, Jess. Wish me luck." I gave her a quick hug.

"Let's go. We have a long two weeks ahead of us," I said as I walked up to Cole.

"You really want to start now?" he asked. "I thought I'd take you out on a date."

"Let's go, Mr. Dakota," I said, pressing. I didn't want to talk about that in front of my coworkers.

"Cole," he insisted.

"Let's go, Mr. Dakota," I repeated, but laughed on the inside.

As we stepped out of the building into the open air, I looked up. All I saw was a beautiful, crystal blue sky. It had rained the night before. The air was a little moist for autumn. I felt the chill in the air as the wind blew past. But no cloud was to be seen as I just stared up at the heavens.

I sometimes wondered why I was there, in New York City. My family lived twenty minutes away, out of the city. *Why am I here and living this life? Why was I chosen to escort Cole Dakota and write an article about him?*

"Crystal Ann?"

I slowly came from my daydreams as I looked over at Cole. "Yes, Mr. Dakota?"

"Are you all right? You just spaced off."

"I like the smell of rain. Especially in a bustling city where all you can smell is the gasoline fumes from cars."

Cole smiled. "The smell of rain is nice. I agree."

"Shall we head on? Where to first?" I asked. I started writing down that he liked the smell of rain on my notepad.

"Lunch."

I took a peek at my watch. *It's definitely lunch time.* "All right, lead on, then."

"Where do you want to go?"

"There's a delicious deli down a few blocks. That would be a good place to start," I said. *Nice and cheap, at least for my wallet.*

"Sounds good," he replied.

We walked in silence. The wind sang past our ears, keeping us entertained. As we entered the deli, I noticed that he wasn't recognized immediately. People were so entertained by technology and by others that they didn't seem to notice or care.

"It doesn't happen often," he whispered.

"What doesn't?" I asked in the same voice.

"Them all *not* running up to me and asking for an autograph. They're too busy twiddling their thumbs to notice me." He winked.

Cole sat down at a table away from the window as I ordered two sandwiches from the deli worker at the counter. I sat down and began to watch for our food.

"Aren't you going to take notes about how I eat?"

"I don't think that matters at all."

"It does in the daily routine of my life," he laughed.

"I guess I am surprised that you're eating at a deli that doesn't have any Michelin stars. I am guessing you probably eat gourmet every night."

"Not all the time. I sometimes make my own food for dinner."

"Oh, how interesting. You can cook?"

"You gonna write that down?"

"No. I'll keep that for my personal entertainment." I grinned mischievously.

*

After dinner, we wandered around the city, much to Cole's entertainment. It was getting late, and we had pretty much done nothing worthy of an article the whole day. My feet were feeling the pain from wearing heels.

"It's getting late. How long do you expect me to follow you around?" I asked.

"My hours are before the sun rises and after the sun sets."

"What time do you want me to pick you up?" I asked with a sigh. *Waking up early sounds dreadful; I really hope he won't make me do that.*

"I will pick you up. I'll need your address," he smiled.

"No. I will follow you back to your hotel, and I will go there to meet you. I am not taking you back to my apartment." It was my final answer, and I was putting my foot down.

He gave me a disappointed look, then looked toward the darkening sky. "Is it because you don't want me to see how cool your place is?"

No, it's actually very dirty and messy. I wonder if Cole knows that girls can be just as dirty, or even more dirty than boys can. I gave him my stern look. I held my tongue, not wanting to say that my apartment was a mess.

"All right, fine." he finally said. "But I deserve something in return."

"What do you want?" I asked.

"How about a phone number, huh?"

I blushed slightly; his eyes sparkled as they looked at me. I was being put under his spell, so I quickly looked away. "No. You'll have to earn that," I said. "I know you like me."

"I do? I didn't know I'd like someone like you," he said coldly.

I raised my eyebrows, my blush disappearing. "Sorry. . . for misunderstanding," I said, suddenly uncomfortable.

He laughed. "Don't worry. I think you're cute, and I definitely want dibs on you."

I was surprised and slightly disappointed that he didn't like me. I looked at his hands.

"Suddenly becoming silent now?"

I didn't answer as I saw his pinkie slightly twitch, and then my pinkie finger felt like it was being pulled toward Cole's hand. A flicker of red came into view and quickly disappeared with the setting sun.

"Crystal Ann, did I hurt your feelings?" He put his hand onto my shoulders and leaned toward me in a kind way.

"Oh, no," I said as I looked up at him, a little dazed. "Your words didn't hurt at all. Although, you could've put it in a better way."

He grinned. "There you are. You dozed off."

"I do that a lot," I said as I turned away, letting his hands fall from me. "Let's get to your hotel."

"Oh, right. It's almost night-break."

"What?" I asked.

"It's like daybreak but it's night-break instead." He turned to lead me.

I giggled and shook my head in disbelief, following behind him.

After ten minutes of walking or so, we came upon his hotel. It was beautiful. A person who could afford to stay here wouldn't have to worry about money.

"You wanna see inside?" he asked.

"Yes. But only because I want to see how luxurious it is." I tried to hide the fact that I was jealous. I really wanted to go inside the fancy hotel just to say I had been inside without being kicked out for loitering.

"You really just wanna see inside, don't you?"

"Let's not go there. C'mon." I pushed him forward as we stepped inside.

These floors were made from pure granite, I'm guessing. It is so smooth and polished I can see my reflection in the floors. You could eat off these clean floors. I saw the walls were filled with beautiful art and the ceilings lined with crystal chandeliers that were probably plated with real gold.

"Wow," I whistled as I looked around. As I gawked at the place around me, Cole pulled me forward toward the front desk.

"Can I help you, Mr. Dakota?" asked the man at the desk.

"I was wondering if I could get a key to my room for my friend here?"

"Will she be staying with you?" the man asked.

Cole leaned toward him. "Not most nights, as she likes to sleep in her own bed. If you know what I mean."

"Cole!" I said as I smacked his arm.

"Ha! You called me Cole!"

"Mr. Dakota, please, don't give me a key to your room. I won't need it," I said.

"It's no problem, Crystal Ann. Or, Ms. Alston."

"I can't really give a key out to someone who isn't going to stay in your room, sir," the man said discreetly.

"Oh, please, man. She has to follow me around everywhere, and she won't give me her address to pick her up. I had to tell her where I am staying, and I know you won't let her go past the elevator without a key. What if I want her to meet me in my room?" he asked.

"Sorry, sir," the man said awkwardly, now trying to avoid eye contact.

"Mr. Dakota, I'll just meet you here in the lobby each morning. It's no big deal. I can wait." I said.

Cole sighed as he rolled his eyes. "Fine," he said. He stood up straight and turned away from the man. "Meet me here at 6 a.m."

"6 a.m.?! I don't even have to get up that early for work."

"Hmm," he said. "You'll have to wake up early. You're on a superstar's schedule now."

I sighed and rolled my eyes. I moaned and crossed my arms over my chest. "I'll meet you here at 6 a.m. then."

"Great! See you then," he exclaimed. "You don't need me to call a taxi?"

"No. I'll be fine." I turned away.

"I'll see you tomorrow, Crystal Ann Alston."

"Goodbye, Cole Dakota," I said mockingly. I left the hotel and made my way home.

Chapter Four

I arrived at his hotel a few minutes before six. I looked at my watch as the second hand ticked ever so slowly. I walked into the hotel as confidently as I could, pushing my slightly messy hair back. It didn't want to work with me this morning, not at all.

"Are you Ms. Alston?" a man asked, as he came up to me.

"That's me." He was the same man as yesterday.

"Mr. Dakota—Cole is waiting for you in his room," he said as he motioned for me to follow him. I wondered why I had to go up to his room. *It better be because he's sick, and I get a paid day off today.*

I followed the man into the elevators. It was awkward— at least for me—standing next to him as the elevator music went on without any conversation. *I really hate the elevator sometimes; I prefer to ride the elevator by myself. I'm not sure if I can sit in comfortable silence with anyone. Thinking back, though, there was a comfortable silence between Cole and me.*

"You all right?" the man asked as he looked back at me.

"Oh, yeah, I'm fine. I just go into my mind a lot." I laughed nervously as I waved him off.

We stopped at the 30th floor of the building. The elevator opened to a suite. "I have a quick question before I get out," I said to the bellhop.

"Yes?"

"Why do I have to have a key when the elevator leads right to the suite?"

"To get into the elevator, ma'am, you need to scan the key and go to the right floor automatically," the man said with a curt nod. "Here you are, ma'am," he added, leading me with his motion out of the elevator.

"Thank you," I said, nodding.

As I walked into the suite, I smelled a sweet smell, like sweet eggs. My mouth began to water. Drool dripped down my chin, but I quickly wiped it away. *They smell so good. I didn't have time to make myself breakfast this morning.* I wandered into the suite as the delicious scent of bacon came to my nose. I could tell the bacon wasn't burnt. *It's nicely crisp but chewy at the same time.*

I put a hand to my mouth to calm my drool and myself down.

"Oh, Crystal Ann!" I heard Cole say as I walked into the kitchen.

"Mr. Dakota." As I turned my head, my eyes beheld his bare chest. He had a perfectly toned chest, lean and slightly muscled, not a hair in sight. His broad shoulders complemented the rest of his physique. And, he was a lot more tan than I thought he looked yesterday.

I blushed and looked away quickly.

"It's Cole." He came over to me. "Do you want a hug?" he asked playfully. "You look a little hot."

"No, get away from me." I took a few steps forward as he approached from behind.

"Aw. You're embarrassed."

"I'll call you Cole if you put on a shirt." I gave him a sideways glance, seeing his naked chest in the corner of my eye before quickly turning back.

"I don't look that bad, do I?" He laughed as I heard him walk the other way.

My stomach churned as I slowly turned around. He wasn't there. I sighed with relief. *Why would he do that if he knew I was coming? Is he just being a troll? I think he is. He's a mean troll.*

"You came just in time for breakfast," Cole said, coming back down the hall.

"You mean the sweet eggs and the bacon?"

"I take it that you like sweet eggs and bacon." He laughed.

"Yes. My favorite." I nodded.

"Hash browns too."

"Only if they're diced," I said with a little shrug.

"I'll get that some other time for you." He smiled kindly as he looked at me with his baby blue eyes.

I stared into his eyes for a moment as I stood there.

Who is this man? Why is he so mysterious and charming? I already know I like him, a lot. He's rich. Handsome. So. . . sweet, at times.

"Crystal Ann?"

"Yes?" I looked up at him, trying to be more professional.

"Are you all right? You stared at me so—weird." His eyebrow raised in curiosity.

"Sorry! I was off in my mind," I apologized. I quickly looked away to hide my embarrassment. "Let's have you eat breakfast and go."

"Don't you want some?"

"It's your breakfast. I wouldn't want to intrude," I said.

"I am inviting you to eat with me, for one. And two, I know you wanted to see what my suite looked like." He grinned.

I laughed, a bit defeated. He read me so well that I couldn't deny the truth.

He led me over to the table by the terrace. The rising sun made the city glow reds, pinks, oranges, and fading purples. It was almost romantic. Two plates were on the table.

"You planned this?"

"I will not deny that," he said. "We are also going to watch the sun rise."

I felt like face-palming myself. *Oh, Cole Dakota, you are making this seem like a date. What are you doing to my heart? It doesn't hurt, but it beats fast as if it does. This can't happen. You are bound to know that.*

My eyes met his as the sun continued to take its time to rise. The oranges glowing around us suited him well. *Can we work?*

"It's been a few years since I've seen the sunrise from a skyscraper like this." I looked away from him, letting my train of thought crash and burn. I sat down at the table as calmly as I could.

"I'll be right back," he said, watching me sit down and stare out into the city. He came back with two fancy serving trays covered in silver lid domes.

He opened up the tray next to me and the food was steaming hot. The smell hit my nose, and my mouth began to water so much more. He moved the empty plate away and gave me a plate of sweet eggs and bacon.

"Some wine?" he asked, as he picked up orange juice.

"That's not wine," I laughed at his tease, rolling my eyes.

"It's wine," he winked as he poured the orange juice into two champagne glasses.

This man is too sweet.

"Enjoy," he said. "Just don't go and get drunk on me."

I rolled my eyes and picked up the fork. I stared at the eggs and bacon with a solemn expression.

"Crystal Ann, I can tell you haven't eaten breakfast," Cole said. "You should eat."

"How can you tell that?" I asked, raising an eyebrow to call out his bluff.

"Well, to start, you were still yawning when you came up here. You also didn't smell of food. I was close enough to smell your horrible Colgate toothpaste that tries to smell of mint but doesn't," he said.

I was surprised and tried to hide my sadness at his comment about my inexpensive toothpaste.

"You didn't know I could do that, huh?" He grinned, leaning toward me.

"No, I'm just sorry you had to smell my toothpaste, the way you described it . . ." I felt awkward and definitely embarrassed.

Cole laughed out loud as he leaned back in his chair. For some reason, it helped me feel a little bit better.

"No worries. It just tells me you're tight on money and that's probably why you took this gig. You probably told your boss you want more money for these two weeks."

"Interesting conclusion," I said, trying to hide my guilt as I took a bite of the food.

"That is also why you don't eat breakfast, but I know you're hungry," he said.

"As I said," I responded, "interesting conclusion."

Cole smiled as he began to eat his food. "Are you Christian?"

"Does that matter?"

"No, of course not. I am just interested if you believe in a God that looks down at you from above, watching your every move and will be there when you mess up."

I almost choked on my food as I swallowed. *He's making this seem like an interrogation.*

"You make him sound so much like a . . . creep when you put it that way," I said, a bit uncomfortable with the description. "I would say I believe in God or a higher being," I continued, "although, I feel like he or she or it has abandoned me." I shrugged.

"That's . . . that's too bad, Crystal Ann." He nodded a little bit at my answer. His eyes glowed with a sad expression.

"Thanks?" I shoved more food into my mouth. He didn't speak more of the subject as we continued to eat. We ate in silence.

"Thanks for the food," I said as I pushed myself away from the table.

"You're welcome," he nodded. "You ate fast. You must've been hungry."

I shrugged as I leaned back into my chair and looked down at my hands. I heard Cole put his silverware down. I *felt* his stare.

"I'd like if you didn't stare at me," I whispered.

"I can't help but wonder if you're really okay," he said sincerely.

I blinked as my hazel eyes stared right into his blue eyes. "I am a reporter, and I am here to report on you. My feelings don't matter, Cole." I cleared my throat, gaining my composure back. I sat up straight in my chair.

Cole smiled and shook his head slightly. "If you say so, Crystal Ann."

"Just tell me when you're done eating." I stood up from the table. "Excuse me." He nodded toward the nice white couches that were facing a huge television.

I sat down as I looked through my Facebook newsfeed on my phone. I saw people I knew from high school getting married, having children, graduating from college with a master's. *I am missing out on so many things.*

I put my phone down, and I noticed Cole looking right at me.

"Are you done eating? We can get a move on with our day, if you are," I said as I sat up straight.

"No, not yet. I just wanted to see what your face looks like when you're looking at your phone."

"I didn't know that people made a face while they looked at their phone." I was intrigued.

"They're mostly blank stares. Followed by a few little grins. I just wanted to see if you had a pretty face." He winked, looking back at me for a moment.

"Sure. Finish your breakfast."

"All right. I will, then." He chuckled.

*

After Cole finished his breakfast and got dressed, we headed down the elevator. As we stepped in together, Cole put his arm around me. "What are we going to do first?" he questioned.

"Hmm." I leaned into his shoulder, teasing him. "What do you want to do?"

"Central Park? I heard there might be a concert going on." He brought his face closer to mine.

"Oh?" I did not let up. *I want him to surrender at least once to this closeness.* "What would we do at a concert that would be relevant to me writing the article about you?"

"Maybe, that behind the scene, I live a seemingly normal life. At least, the most normal life that I can have," he said. He moved his arms with exaggeration as he put an arm back over my shoulders.

I pulled away. Cole raised his eyebrows and gave me weird look. I looked at the elevator doors as we continued to go down. The elevator dinged quietly at every passing floor level. I closed my eyes and took in a deep breath.

"Inside your mind again?" Cole questioned.

"Oh," I said as I looked up at him. "Yes. I drift off a lot."

"That better not stop you from working," Cole teased.

I folded my arms a little below my chest. "I could say the same for you. I thought you were working on a movie."

"Yeah, I was," Cole confirmed with a small nod.

"Aren't you still filming here in New York if you haven't flown back yet?"

Cole shrugged as the elevator dinged loudly and the doors opened. We walked out of the elevator and into the lobby of the hotel.

"You're taking a long time to answer me," I said as we walked through the lobby.

"Because, it's something to ponder. The movie is done, for the most part. My role is done, at least. The movie is coming out in about a year. Most of the crew is back in California because filming is finished. Now, it's on to the editing," he said. We arrived at the front doors, and a doorman opened them for us.

"Thank you," Cole and I said at the same time. The doorman gave us a smile and nod as we walked out into the brisk morning air.

I stopped and gave him a look of suspicion. "Why are you here, then?"

"Come, let's move on from this conversation," he said.

I straightened. "Why?"

Cole just laughed at me as he grabbed my hand and tugged me along. "Come on, Crystal Ann, let's go," he said, ignoring my question completely.

I rolled my eyes as I followed him. We wandered down the street, coming upon all the boutiques. As we walked past several different shops, I spotted a gorgeous dress in a window shop. It was a deep forest green A-line dress. It had a deep neckline that showed some cleavage, and there was a slit from the right mid-thigh. The long sleeves on the dress complemented it well along with another piece of the same colored fabric that wrapped around the waist of the dress. From the drape of the skirt, it looked like the fabric was chiffon. I stopped and gawked at it with a small smile.

"It looks too elegant for your budget," Cole commented.

"It is. But it doesn't hurt to dream." I slowly continued to walk beside Cole. *I bet the dress doesn't even come in a size 10.*

Central Park was already flooded with people, as usual.

"Let's hurry to the gazebo."

"Why?" Cole asked. "We don't even have a blanket yet."

"You really want to sit down on a blanket, like it's a picnic?" I chuckled. "New York isn't the city of lovers."

"Of course not! That's Paris. But, where in the grass would we sit?"

"That's all part of the magic, isn't it?"

Cole rolled his eyes at my comeback. He smiled. "Oh, wait," he blurted out.

"What?" I curtly questioned.

"The concert doesn't start until sundown." Cole looked at me with an evil grin.

"What do we do in the meantime, then?" I asked, becoming a little impatient.

"I don't know. Window shop?" he questioned.

"I have never heard a man say they want to go shopping before," I chuckled. I felt my frustration suddenly release itself when he said he wanted to go shopping.

"Well, as long as it's with a beautiful girl, I guess I'm all right with doing whatever she wants to do," Cole said smoothly.

I was definitely uncertain of this man's taste in women. "All right, but we're not going window shopping. We're going to do an interview."

"What," Cole uttered. "I got you for two weeks. An interview on the first day?" He made a small pouting face and looked at me with sad eyes.

"I don't usually try to play on the job," I revealed with a little sass.

"That is my job." He smiled at me again.

"I would've figured that you'd have other people go shopping for you." I shrugged, crossing my arms over my chest again.

"Some do," he spoke truthfully.

"Let's go find a bench." I began to walk to the nearest one.

"Can we at least feed pigeons as you interview me?"

"Fine." I rolled my eyes at the request.

***

We sat down on a bench in the shade of a big saucer magnolia, its leaves already falling.

Cole threw some birdseed onto the sidewalk as pigeons watched in awe. A few flew down and began to peck at the ground. I watched them for a moment before I brought out my notepad and pen from the breast pocket of my jacket.

"Ha! So that's where it was this whole time," Cole said, his eyes sparkling.

"I didn't know you were looking for it."

"Would you have shown it to me either way?" he asked.

"That's beside the point," I retorted in a higher pitch. "Let's begin."

A woman walked up to us as I was about to ask the first question for the interview. "You're Cole Dakota, aren't you?" the woman asked in a giddy voice.

"That I am, ma'am. What can I do you for?" he asked in a charming way.

My face flushed from embarrassment. *I don't know why I am feeling like this. I guess it's because I am walking around with a major star. I'm not too sure.* My heart beat wildly as Cole's and the lady's conversation drew on.

"Crystal Ann, could I borrow a page of your notebook? This young lady doesn't have a piece of paper on her," Cole asked.

"Sure." I ripped out a page for her to use, also handing Cole my pen.

"Thank you, Crys."

I gave Cole a look. He was being very familiar with me in front of this woman. I looked away from Cole and at the woman. She looked so happy and excited to meet Cole in real life. Her eyes never wandered over to me.

"Was I interrupting something?" the woman asked suddenly as she saw me staring at her.

"Crys?" Cole looked at me for a moment as he autographed the page with a note to the woman.

"It's Crystal Ann, please," I said as kindly as I could to Cole, trying to be professional. "No, you weren't interrupting. I have two weeks to interview this guy, but he luckily evades it all the time." The words slipped out of my mouth.

"Sorry," she said with an awkward chuckle. "I can go."

"No worries," I squeaked. "It's not every day you see *the* Cole Dakota, right?"

I saw Cole's expression turn to a surprised one.

"I can leave you two alone, if you'd like," I offered. I stood up, taking my pen back from Cole, putting my notepad and pen back into my breast pocket.

"Really?" the lady exclaimed, obviously excited.

"Cole is really awesome. I am sure he'd love to talk to you more." I began to walk away.

"Crystal Ann," Cole tried to call when the crazed fan sat next to him.

I turned back and gave him my most evil grin.

"I'm going to get me some tea," I shouted as I waved goodbye to him and walked away.

I wandered off, back onto the street and to a Starbucks that was close by. I grabbed some hot tea before making my way back. The wind began to pick up and brought in a cool breeze. I sat down at a picnic table, not too far from where Cole sat with his fan. They were still talking. I brought out my phone and began to read the news. *So much political ruin from everyone with stupid events. Like every day. I wish there was more happy news in the world.*

I sighed as I put my phone down and sipped at my tea. My eyes wandered around at the beauty of Central Park. *A beautiful forest right in the middle of a concrete jungle. It's pretty amazing.* I closed my eyes for only a moment when I heard someone taking a seat next to me.

"You know, you could get mugged easily by snoozing off, and we wouldn't want that."

"I wasn't snoozing off, just enjoying the breeze, Cole." I turned my head to see a man with black hair and piercing brown eyes before me.

"Is that man your new boyfriend? Cole or whatever?" asked Mike, a not so very nice young man I knew from high school. He was a popular boy who was a bit of a player and a *jerk* to me.

"No. I am interviewing him." I turned toward Mike. "It's been a few years since high school."

"Yeah, it has been," he said with a laugh that moved his whole chest up, then he hunched back down. "What have you been doing? What kind of job do you have?"

I looked around and saw a lot of strange men close by. They all had guns.

"I work as a reporter," I spluttered, trying to remain calm. These men looked tough and a gut feeling told me to flee.

"Oh, how interesting. Have you gotten married yet?" He moved closer to me.

"What have you gotten yourself into, Mike?" I asked softly.

"None of your business." Mike said. "I just have some debts to pay, and I thought a pretty girl like you would suffice."

"You're still as crude as ever," I sneered as I began to stand up.

"I wouldn't recommend that," Mike said as he took my hand.

I turned to slap him but I smelled a familiar scent—a pleasant one.

"Crystal Ann Alston, how could you leave me stranded like that?" Cole spoke in a strained voice. "I hate it when you wander off without me."

"I'm sorry, Cole," I muttered. As Mike let go of my hand, I grabbed onto Cole.

"You got some tea?" Cole asked me.

"Yeah," I said as I stared at Mike. He didn't seem to recognize Cole, but, if I remembered right, Mike wasn't a big movie fan.

"Don't forget your phone," Cole said.

"Yeah," I said, watching Mike carefully as I grabbed my phone and my tea from the picnic table, letting Cole escort me away.

We walked away in silence, and I let out a quiet sigh of relief. A bead of sweat fell down the side of my face.

"Who was that man?" Cole asked.

"His name is Mike. He was an acquaintance from high school." I breathed, feeling a mix of malice and concern for Mike. *What was he into? Was he going to kidnap me? Maybe my imagination is overactive.*

"What did he want?"

I took a peek back at Mike as Cole talked to me. Mike was still staring at me intensely. The men with guns grabbed his arms roughly and got him up from the table and escorted him away.

"He's probably a druggie, and it seems like he got himself into some trouble. He thought he could offer me up as a bargain," I scoffed.

"The nerve!" I could see fire come to his eyes as our eyes met. As I held onto his arm with my free hand, I felt his muscle tighten in indignation.

"Yes. The nerve of him." I rolled my eyes, looking away from Cole. "Although, I feel a little bad that he's in that situation."

Cole stopped as he turned me toward him ever so gently. He stared at me with a sad and serious look. "Don't have empathy for a man who got himself into that kind of trouble. The reason why I am who I am today is because I had to behave well to have my reputation built, and I had to work hard. Now, I will admit I have made mistakes, yes, but you shouldn't feel bad for the mistakes I've made in the past and for the mistakes I will make in the future because they're of my own doing. Just like this guy, Mike, you say is his name. Don't you be going around and feeling bad for him when he was going to give you to his buddies in the blink of an eye or a snap of a finger and get off scot-free. No. Crystal Ann, do not feel bad for him. It's his own fault. Nobody deserves sympathy or empathy when their intent is to do something bad."

My eyes widened in surprise as our eyes locked on each other's. I nodded as I looked down at the concrete below me. I was speechless. My pinkie suddenly began to twitch. I gently touched my little finger and felt something like string. I looked again, surprised, seeing a red flash before it disappeared.

"How did you ever find me?" I was trying to get what I just saw out of my mind.

"I have a homing-sense for people I would like to keep close. That, and I saw you weren't too far away from where I was sitting with my fan," he said with a little grin.

"Homing-sense?"

"Yeah, like a homing pigeon." He made movements that were supposed to represent a pigeon.

I laughed out loud as I shook my head at him. "You're silly." I turned away from him. "But, finding me . . . it had to be more by chance. I'm pretty sure a tree was in the way of us seeing one another."

We began to walk again. "Maybe. Most likely, but I would like my homing-sense be the story."

"If it'll help you sleep at night." I shrugged with a grin.

I felt a twinge of pain in my pinky again. *It's been on and off for the past few days now. Is something wrong with my hand? Maybe I have been writing or typing too much for my own good.* I glanced down at my hand. *It looks normal.*

Cole took my tea from my hand and sipped at it. "Wow, green tea."

"What?" I questioned, my attention moving off my pinkie.

"I'd rather have something less . . . " Cole started.

"Herbal?"

"I guess you could put it that way," Cole said as he continued to try and to think of another way to put what he was going to say in words. "Why is English such a hard language?"

I started to mentally doze off as I looked at my pinkie again. A flash of fire red went past my eyes, like the sun's reflection off of a shiny surface. I shook my head slightly and gently touched my pinkie to subdue the pain. It worked for a bit. It felt like my pinkie was being pulled off.

"Crystal Ann, you've got to stop dozing off on me." Cole placed my tea back into my hand.

"Sorry, I can't seem to help myself," I said. I took the slightly colder cup into my hands and sipped. *My tea is lukewarm. It's kinda gross now.* I sighed as we passed a garbage can, and I tossed away my tea.

"You sure you're all right?" Cole asked.

"Yes, I am fine. Just a little tired. Had an early start to my day." I stretched my shoulders a bit.

"Well, I could give you a massage," he said.

"No," I said playfully. "I am perfectly fine, and I personally don't want you touching me in that way."

Cole stepped back a little bit. "Sorry," he apologized.

I sighed. "I was being playful," I said, a little impatient.

His eyes sparkled as he looked down at me. "Really? Crystal Ann, being playful with me?"

"Don't get used to it," I teased, pushing his chest away from me.

We both laughed as we continued walking.

"Just don't leave me again, Crystal Ann," Cole said, suddenly turning serious.

"Stuff like that doesn't usually happen to me."

"Usually is the key word," Cole said softly. "And that was mean of you to leave me like that. I ended up having to ditch a fan."

"But, using people as an excuse to get away isn't a right thing to do either," I retorted.

Cole scoffed. "You got me there," he said with a small shrug. "So, where are we going?"

"I thought we were window shopping," I grinned.

"Oh, so play before work?" he said as he put his arm over my shoulder. My heart began to race slightly, but I left his arm alone this time.

"If that will get you to work with me, I guess so." I giggled.

"Or are you hiding the truth because I came and scooped you up at the right time to get you away from the scary man?" His hand gently grew tighter around my shoulder. I looked toward his hand then back up to his face.

"If that helps you sleep," I said softly. Our eyes met. His blue eyes looked so sincere. "Should we continue on to window shopping?" I asked softly, disturbing the silence between us.

"Yeah, let's go window shopping." He turned away and withdrew his arm.

"Just window shopping!" I warned. "I don't like to spend money when I've promised to go window shopping."

Cole replied, "Of course. Just window shopping."

"No going inside or anything," I insisted.

"Just looking through the window," he said with a little nod.

Chapter Five

All I see around me is darkness. I feel myself turn my head slightly and hear beautiful classical music playing in front of me. My back and neck feel so warm. I turn around to see a light cracking through a door. I walk toward it at a slow pace and the door slowly opens.

My eyes opened and I saw people sitting in front of me, some on blankets and others on chairs. My pillow was a pair of legs that were stretched out across a fluffy blanket and a hand was rubbing my back.

I moaned as I looked up to see Cole smiling down at me. The final notes of the last song gently flowed through the air as our eyes met.

"Did you sleep nicely?" His eyes were kind.

"I think so," I whispered as I sat up. "Is it over?"

"Yeah. You fell asleep a few songs in, but your mind seemed to be gone even before the concert. You looked as if you were spaced out."

"I must've been really tired," I pulled my hair back, stretched, and yawned. "I'm sorry I slept through the whole thing."

"No worries. I loved hearing the music. Even if you weren't fully listening, you probably heard the music in your sleep and the applause."

A chilled breeze brushed past us. I groaned as I shivered.

Cole helped me up and put the blanket over my shoulders. The body heat from both of us warmed me up quickly.

"You still seem really out of it," he said. "You sure you didn't partake of any alcohol?"

I smiled and shook my head. "I am not that kind of girl. I personally think alcoholic drinks smell like piss."

He was silent for a moment. "That's an interesting way to put it, but it's an agreeable reason. Beer does smell like that."

I sighed as we walked through Central Park. The night sky was dark and the only light came from the lamps surrounding the park.

"Do you want me to escort you to your apartment?"

"Who said I lived in an apartment?" I asked back.

"Just figured. You're a beautiful girl that obviously doesn't have a boyfriend or any other family watching over her. You don't get many calls, actually, none that I have seen yet. Probably a few texts but those are from work. I secretly think you're lonely," he said.

I gently patted his arm with my hand with a small laugh. "No. I'm not lonely, but other than that, you're spot on. And it's not much of a secret anymore."

"Where's your family?"

"Mostly, out in the country."

"Farmer girl?"

"No. Not exactly. Well, I was a rancher." I said with a small nod.

"Wow, so interesting."

"I feel as if you're saying that sarcastically." I raised an eyebrow at him.

He chuckled. "Nah. Well, maybe. You seem to know me all too well." He gave me a wink as we continued down the sidewalk. "What brought you out to the city?"

"Even though I loved growing up with animals where it was nice and quiet, I knew that ranching was something I didn't want to do," I said simply. "Why did you want to become an actor?"

"You really want to know?" Cole chuckled.

"Yeah, I do."

"Well," he said as he gave a small smile. "Even when I was little, I loved being in plays and on center-stage. But, my father soon couldn't stand me being in all these skits and plays because my mother passed away when I was younger. My father was depressed and didn't want to go anywhere after he came home from work. So I started to create them myself and post them on YouTube.

"As I was doing that, I was taking a lot of drama classes in high school, and the drama teacher, bless her heart, let me be in the plays at school for free because she knew of my financial situation. My drama teacher was a great teacher; she was so kind and nice. She was like a mother to me. She had a talent scout come out to one of our plays and he really, really liked me and he recruited me for a movie.

"I finished high school at sixteen and was homeschooled on the side while I went on to become the actor I am today. I did, however, make sure to pay what generosity was shown to me forward for the drama department there. I fund every play and see every play that comes out of that high school. Some of the best years of my life."

I took out my notepad and wrote down a few notes.

"So this was a sneaky way to get in an interview question?" His small smile turning into a big one.

"Got to get them in somehow." I smiled. "It was a nice dream that you had. Do you still have the videos up on YouTube?"

He grinned. "Are you gonna say that in your article?"

"No. I would just like to watch them myself. See if you made a fool of yourself on the internet before you had agents to stop you," I joked. I pressed my lips lightly together in wonder.

His smile only seemed to get bigger as he laughed out loud. "I'll show them to you sometime. How about that?"

I nodded. "I almost feel as if you won't do it."

He rolled his eyes with a chuckle. "It's just a little embarrassing, I guess."

"You guess? I would've never known a celebrity would second guess on any of their actions," I teased.

He sighed as he stopped and looked toward the ground.

"Are you all right?" I asked.

"The way you tease me sometimes doesn't feel like teasing at all," he said with a slight laugh.

"Oh," I said softly. "I'm sorry. I don't mean it that way."

"Got you!" he jeered. A big smile came to his face.

"You were acting, weren't you?" I asked.

"I was," he laughed. "You looked so serious. You were almost cute."

"Almost?"

"Yes, almost," he winked.

Soon, we arrived at his hotel. I was saying my goodbyes when he invited me for dinner.

"I am fine without a late dinner." I laughed, but he had a serious look in his eyes.

"Would you have dinner with me, Crystal Ann?" His smile was kind as he held out his hand toward me.

I grinned. "Let's not make it a habit. Don't want it to look like I am taking advantage of you."

He chuckled. "Of course not."

We went up to his apartment where dinner was already waiting for the both of us. "You knew that I just can't resist good food, huh?" I asked casually.

"I don't think anyone can," Cole said as he led me to the table.

"When did you have time to do this?" I asked as he helped me into my seat.

"The fan that you left me with had to go. So, I decided to call the hotel before I went to find you. You weren't too far away."

He lifted a platter with lobster. My mouth began to drool as I saw how glorious and red it was. As I ate the lobster, the flavor gently melted on my tongue and slipped down my throat with an amazing buttery taste that was too good for words.

"I am guessing you don't have these nights often?" he asked.

"I really don't," I spoke as I ate more.

I finally pushed my plate aside and yawned. "The dinner was very good, but I should be heading home now."

Cole stood up with me. "Let me walk you to the door then."

"Thank you."

He pressed the elevator button. "You're welcome. It's always fun to work with a fun person."

The elevator dinged open as it arrived. "I can agree with that," I said. "But I don't know if you're such a fun person yet."

He scoffed, feigning hurt as he put a hand to his chest. "I'm hurt, Crystal Ann."

"It's not like you would want me to kiss it better," I retorted.

"Probably not, but who says I wouldn't want one anyway?"

"Sounds like you're thirsty and desperate. See you tomorrow morning before the sun rises, Cole Dakota," I said as the elevator door closed.

"I'll see you later," Cole whispered before the elevator door closed all the way. I descended to the main floor.

I can't fall for him. Our lifestyles could never meld. He could never love someone as normal as me. I'm too plain to be any superstar's significant other.

Chapter Six

Before going to meet Cole this morning, I cooked myself some breakfast while listening to the radio. Perhaps I wanted to prove Cole wrong about me starving myself because I'm poor.

"A woman by the name of Helen Parker has been missing since yesterday morning. If you have any information, please contact the police," the radio announcer said. I shook off the feeling that it was caused by Mike, who wasn't looking too good yesterday. I could tell he wanted to do some weird things to me, but I didn't know what. I hoped that lady was all right, but I felt guilty.

I took a deep breath and shook the feeling off as I quickly ate my breakfast and got an early start on the day. I headed to Cole's hotel.

I yawned as I entered the doors to the highly lit lobby. I moaned as the granite floor reflected the bright lights, making them even brighter, too bright for a tired girl's eyes to bear.

A bell-boy walked up to me. "Mr. Dakota is waiting for you."

"Is he now?"

"You're Miss Alston, correct?" I nodded as I yawned and stretched. "Please, let me escort you to the elevator, Miss Alston," the boy said kindly.

"Thank you," I yawned again as he opened up the elevator for me.

"You're welcome, Miss Alston." He nodded to me as the elevator door closed.

As the elevator dinged open, I heard the shower running and saw breakfast for two on the table. I grinned.

"Cole?" I spoke loudly as I walked over and sat on the couch. I assumed he couldn't hear me over the shower.

I brought out my notepad and began to doodle. I thought of Cole's smiling face staring down at me with his enchanting eyes, and I drew him on my small notepad.

"Oh," Cole said behind me. "Crystal Ann, you're early today."

I hadn't noticed Cole coming out of his room with only pants on, his chest still glistening with water.

I looked up and put my hand over my doodle to hide it. "Yes. I also already had my breakfast today." I grinned.

"Aw, I see. Why did you decide to eat breakfast this morning?"

"I figured I should feed myself this morning." I went back to my doodle.

"Aw man, I thought we were gonna have breakfast together again," he playfully whined.

"Well, not every day should be the same." I yawned again. "Wow, I am yawning a lot this morning," I mumbled.

"You still tired? You could doze off as I eat my unusually large breakfast," Cole teased. He walked over to the table, sat down in front of a plate, and began to eat.

"That was your own fault for not asking." I felt sassy.

"I don't have your number to ask," he said.

"That would be a dream. . . to get *your* number."

"Why's that?" he asked.

"I would sell it on eBay." I grinned as I looked up at him for a moment.

He laughed out loud as he stuffed more food in his mouth. "That would be a great way to make money. I should do that more often."

"Sell your phone number?" I laughed.

"It would be a great investment in myself."

"I guess, if you wanted. I'll write that down," I teased.

"How would that relate to your article?"

"Well, I could start off by saying that you're a big tease and to watch for your number on auction websites because they might be the real deal."

We both laughed.

Cole continued to eat as I doodled the rest of my picture of him. I looked at my masterpiece. It was a beautiful little *doodle* of him, though not a very good sketch; he looked cartoonish.

He was behind me with his arm over my shoulder. "So, what are you doing?" I didn't have enough time to cover my work.

"Nothing, really." I put my hand over my notepad.

"Did you doodle me?" His voice raised to a higher pitch with pleasure. His eyes were wide as he grabbed my notepad from me. I felt my cheeks flush red because my drawing skills aren't the best. I stayed silent as he went silent. I swear he didn't breathe for a little bit as he looked at my doodle.

"I know it's bad," I muttered uncomfortably as he looked at it.

"No, it's really not. I like it a lot," he said seriously. "It's better than I could draw in this format."

I looked up at him with a raised eyebrow. "This format?" I smiled.

"Well, I draw more realistically than this. I look animated."

"That's the point," I said and nodded my head.

"But, I like it a lot. I am going to keep it," he said.

"Who said you could?" I intervened by grabbing my notepad. "I haven't even signed my work yet."

"Oh," he said. "That's true. You should sign it and give it to me."

"Hmm, what would you do for it?" I asked.

"Not much. Just take the awesome portrait of me from you." He shrugged.

I shook my head. "Fine. I guess you're gonna get it one way or another." I signed my name, ripped the picture out of my notepad, and gave it to him.

"It really is awesome," Cole repeated.

"I sure hope so." I looked over and realized he still didn't have a shirt on. I blushed as I looked away. *He has a really nice body*. "S-So," I started, "Do you want to do anything specific today?"

"Playing on the job?" he suggested.

I laughed, loosening up. "Well, that's what you do, and I have to do what you want to do for these two weeks, pretty much."

Cole laughed. "All right. What do you want to do?"

"That's not for me to decide." I looked up into Cole's eyes.

"Statue of Liberty?"

"If that's what you want to do."

A big grin came to his lips as he stood up. He stretched while standing. "Let me grab a shirt then," he said.

I sighed as I sat back in the couch and closed my eyes. *This feels so unreal. I wonder why Cole is doing this. I know I am starting to fall for him because he is obviously a man girls can't help but fall in love with. This is so frustrating. I really don't want to get hurt when I get rejected.* I opened my eyes to see his face above mine.

"Crystal Ann?" Cole asked. "You all right?"

"Yeah, just a little tired. Let's head out, then." I yawned. "We'll have to catch a ferry out there, so it'll be a few hours. Do you want to buy snacks?" I asked.

"No. I'll be fine," he said. "I had a very big breakfast."

I laughed as we went down the elevator and out of the building.

"Let's get a taxi," I suggested.

"We could walk," he said.

"That'd take even more than just a few hours, and we wouldn't want you to be in pain because you need your legs for acting," I teased.

"You have a point." Cole playfully pouted as I hailed a taxi.

As I told the taxi driver to take us to the Statue of Liberty, my phone rang. "Hello, this is Crystal Ann."

"Hi, Crysie," my mom said over the line.

"Hey, Mom," I said, smiling ear to ear. "There something you need?"

"Your sister Lyndsay Ana is moving back home, and we need your help. Can you take the day off today?"

I shook my head, sighing in disappointment. "I am actually with my job right now."

"What is it?" Cole asked quietly.

"It's nothing," I said kindly to Cole. "But, I can try and help later."

"Maybe he'd like to help," Mom said. "Or is she a she?"

"No, he's a he," I confirmed. "But I wouldn't want to ask that of him."

Suddenly, Cole took the phone from my hands. "Hi, this is Cole, Crystal Ann's friend. There something you need?" he asked kindly with a big grin on his face.

I gave him a little pout and a raise of my eyebrow.

"Give that back," I demanded.

His eyes lit up. He nodded and every once in a while spoke, "Uh-huh . . . yeah."

"What are you doing?" I asked in a soft voice.

"Driver, can we go to a different location instead?" Cole asked.

"Where to?" the driver asked.

Cole gave him my mother's home address, and the driver smiled. He turned around and headed the opposite way.

"Why are we going there?" I asked as he handed me my phone back.

"Because I'd love to meet your family." Cole winked.

"Hello, Mom?" I asked as I put the phone back to my ear.

"Your friend there is very nice. I can't wait to see you, Crystal Ann! Hugs and kisses!" Mom said before hanging up.

I sighed as I put my phone on my lap.

"Something wrong?" Cole asked.

"I guess I am just kind of nervous," I told him truthfully.

"Hmm," Cole said as he leaned back. "I wonder why."

"My mother can be . . . well, a mother," I said with a small smile. I figured that talking about mothers might upset him, as his mother passed away when he was younger, but speaking with him about my mother didn't seem to be invoking any reaction from him.

"Too . . . what's the word? Overly attached?" he asked.

"She's just going to question you extensively, and she's probably going to recognize you as an actor," I said. "She's a movie-lover."

"I am thinking we're going to get along just great," Cole said.

"Ignore if she says something stupid. I don't bring boys home," I stated.

"Boys?" he asked.

I scoffed as I rolled my eyes. "Men, then. Most of them act like boys, anyways." I pushed back my hair from my face.

"I am guessing you have had bad experiences."

"Doesn't matter," I answered too quickly.

He gave a curt nod as he brought out his phone and took a selfie of himself. He chuckled as he looked at his photo. I shook my head as I saw him typing on Twitter.

"What?" he asked, not looking up.

"I think it's kind of stupid to take a picture of yourself and just post it without any purpose," I admitted.

He gave me a weird expression. Then, he laughed.

"What?" I asked.

"I check in with my fans every once in a while to let them know I'm doing okay. I love to interact with them as much as possible and one of the ways to do that is to post meaningless pictures on social media," he explained.

"I never thought of it that way," I said.

"That, and I'm sure that everyone knows now that a reporter is following me around everywhere and is taking me to her mother's house," he teased.

I shook my head at his teasing. "You're the one that wanted to go. I tried to slip out of going."

"I can't help but want to see the woman that raised you, Crystal Ann. I wonder if she is as weird as you, or even weirder. Maybe, you're trying to cover up the place where you come from."

I laughed out loud as I shook my head. "I guess you'll have to find out and see."

*

We arrived in the countryside after an hour of trying to get out of the city that slowly got busier as the morning went on. I sighed as I dozed off in the back of the taxi.

I opened my eyes when we stopped, and I saw the house where I had grown up and the big barn behind it. I remembered the fields growing alfalfa, and the animals that were there.

"Wow," Cole said with a big smile, looking out the window. "Is this the house you grew up in?"

"Yeah. It is. It's small but beautiful, isn't it?" I opened the door and got out of the taxi.

Cole paid the taxi driver and quickly followed. "I hope I am strong enough to help carry everything," Cole teased.

"You're a man. You can carry anything if you want to," I said with a small grin.

"How sexist of you. I wouldn't have ever guessed you were sexist, Crystal Ann," Cole said, almost looking serious.

"Ha! You've been in worse movies, so I wouldn't be talking," I retorted and shook my head. A smile crossed his face as he shook his head along with me. He knew I was right.

I puffed out a small breath as we headed to the front door. I was just about to open it door when it swung open, and I was suddenly in my mother's arms.

"Oh, Crystal Ann! You should call me and come visit me more!" Mom cried happily as she held me tightly.

"You know I call you every night, and it's expensive for me to come out every week."

"Oh, I know," she said, pulling away. She gazed into my eyes. "So, where's your fri—?" She looked out to see where Cole was, but when their eyes met, she went pale.

"Mom?" I asked. "Mom, are you all right?"

"It's—It's Cole Dakota!" Mom said, almost shouting with glee. "You didn't tell me your friend was Cole Dakota! Oh, Crystal Ann, you're climbing up in the world! Oh, my goodness!" My mother *giggled*.

I blushed and looked away. I was fully embarrassed. I put my hand onto my forehead.

Cole couldn't help but laugh. "It's nice to meet you, Mrs. . . . ?"

"Oh, it's Mrs. Alston, still," Mom giggled. "You didn't tell me he was such a flattering person." She winked at me.

Cole laughed again, unable to stop. "It's not flattery if it's true, Mrs. Alston."

"Okay!" I interrupted as I put my hands up. "Let's wait for Lyndsay's truck to get here, please," I cried as I slipped past Mom and into the house.

The house smelled like it always had. The smell of delicious, fresh fruit pies came to my nose. I lifted up my head to smell them. The house had an aura that surrounded me with a warm feeling, like a big and warm hug from a mother bear. I drew in a shaky breath as I closed my eyes and took in my old house again.

"Is she always like this?" Cole asked my mother.

"Not usually," Mom said.

The moment quickly passed as my eyes popped open. I looked back toward Cole and my mother.

"Well," I said. "I can't help myself if I love pie, especially Mom's homemade cherry pie."

"Homemade?" Cole asked.

"Yes," Mom said. "Have you ever had homemade pie?"

"Yes, but not in a very long time," Cole answered.

"Well, that's not a good answer. Let's go fill your belly with goodies," my mother smiled wide as she began to push him forward.

I felt as if I was eight again as I walked toward the kitchen. It was like I had just come home from a long day at school.

I spotted the fresh pie sitting by the window, cooling off in the breeze that brushed past. I walked up to the pie and felt the pie tin. It was cool enough to touch, but warm on my hands. I picked up the pie and put it on the counter before I grabbed a knife and a few plates. I didn't listen to anything as I cut a perfect slice of pie and turned around with it on the plate. I looked up and saw Cole with a curious look on his face. I handed him the piece of pie.

"I think you should try it," I offered.

Cole gave me a kind smile as he took the plate.

"Thank you," Cole said as he held the plate under his nose and breathed deeply. My mother handed him a fork. "Are you going to join me, Crystal Ann?" Cole asked.

"Your sister won't be here for another ten minutes, I'm sure," Mom said, cutting me a piece. "Eat some pie. You know you've missed my pie." Mom gave me a cute wink before handing me a plate. I sat down next to Cole.

I smiled as I took the first bite of cherry pie I'd had in a very long time. The sweet taste and warm temperature threw me off guard for a moment. I bit into the soft crust sprinkled with sugar. The sour cherries with the sweetened crust was as perfect as I remembered. I realized I'd missed Mom and her cherry pie.

"Woah!" Cole said as he took his first bite. Cole almost shouted. "This is so great! Don't you agree, Crystal Ann? Mrs. Alston, you should come join us."

My mother looked on with a smile. "Since I was invited, I will join then," Mom said as she served herself a slice and sat beside me. "It's been awhile since I've baked a pie," she told me honestly.

"Really?" I asked. "Tastes like you make them every few days still."

"Well, no one is really here to enjoy them with me anymore," she pointed out softly.

"What about Dad?"

"I am sure he and I couldn't eat pie like we used to. We need to eat a bit healthier now that we're older," my mother said in a solemn voice.

"Yeah, you're right." I sat thinking about what Mom said.

The back door opened with a squeak as I looked back and saw my father walking in. "Dad!" I shouted as I put my fork down, ran over to him, and gave him a hug.

"Crystal Ann has always been a daddy's girl," my mother said to Cole.

Cole stood up and walked over to my father. "Hello, I am Cole Dakota. It's nice to meet Crystal Ann's father."

After my father gave me a warm hug, he gave Cole a hard and cold look as he firmly shook Cole's hand. "I'm Jedikiah. My friends call me Jed, but you're not my friend," my father laughed.

Cole laughed with him. "Well, it's nice to meet you, Jedikiah."

"Just Jed." My father winked.

"Jed."

"Crystal Ann, did you bring him home?" Dad asked.

I looked up at him. "Not in the way that you think. He's my job right now."

"How so?" Dad looked confused, almost concerned.

"I am doing a story on what it's like to be a celebrity," I said. "Like, what it's like to be a celebrity for a day."

"You're a celebrity?" my father asked, surprised.

"Yeah." Cole gave my father a small, shy smile.

"Papa isn't as much as a movie junkie as Mom and I are."

"Wow. How did you stumble into my daughter?" my father asked, intrigued.

"I spilled her coffee on her by accident," Cole calmly said.

"You spilled coffee on my daughter?"

"I'm fine, Dad. And it was my iced tea. I had Jess' coffee on the side," I said.

"Yeah, it happened a few days ago," Cole said.

Dad looked right at me. "You all right? Was it too cold?"

"Yes, I'm fine," I sighed. "You worry too much. I figured you should worry about Lyndsay Ana. She's the younger one of us and is married."

"She's married and has a man taking care of her. I have to worry about my first baby," my father teased.

Cole asked, "Your little sister got married?"

"Yeah. She was practically married at sixteen. It was true love at first sight."

"So, like the Red Thread of Destiny?" Cole asked.

"What's that?" Dad and I asked at the same time. Mom looked up to hear the explanation as well.

"It's an old Japanese legend," Cole shrugged. "It's not well-known in the United States."

"You have to tell us now," I laughed as Cole gave a shy chuckle. He seemed a little intimidated by my father.

"Mom!" I heard my sister shout from the open front door.

"Oh! Lyndsay Ana!" Mom said, going to greet my sister. "We've got a special treat for you!" she shouted happily. "Crystal Ann brought home a special guest."

I suddenly became introverted as I slipped away from my father's arm and sat down to eat the rest of my pie.

Mom brought Lyndsay Ana into the room, and she almost screamed as she saw Cole Dakota standing there. Her eyes sparkled and she stared at him intensely. "Is this really him? How did Crystal Ann bring him home?" She sounded disappointed that it was me who brought him home.

"Brought who home?" Her husband, Rhett, stopped in his tracks. "Oh my—" His mouth was fully open; his eyes almost out of his skull. "It's Cole Dakota!"

"Nice to meet you," Cole laughed. "You must be Lyndsay Ana," he said, looking at my sister. He then turned to her husband. "May I ask your name?"

"I'm Rhett Richardson."

Cole took his hand happily as they shook. "Nice to meet you," Cole said.

"Pleasure is mine." Rhett said breathlessly.

I felt Lyndsay's eyes focus on me as Rhett introduced himself. My eyes met hers for a few moments before I looked back at my pie as if it were more interesting.

"Can I talk to you privately?" my sister asked me. I quickly finished my last bite of pie.

"Sure," I said, standing with a mouth full of pie.

"I'll be right here when you come back, Crystal Ann." A serious tone crept into Cole's voice.

Lyndsay and I went into the guest bedroom. "What are you thinking?" she asked in a harsh voice.

"What do you mean? I know what I am doing, unlike you," I snapped.

She folded her arms over her chest. "Inviting a superstar into our home! That could've caused Mama a heart attack! It nearly caused *me* a heart attack, for Pete's sake!" She raised her voice slightly. "Our family isn't the cleanest, and you could've embarrassed us!"

I scoffed, mocking her in the process. I clenched my hands into fists at my sides.

"First things first, Lyndsay Ana. I am working on an article about him. It was his idea for me to do the article, and my boss is running with it. So, you can't criticize me for doing my job, even if that means bringing him home. And Mom won't have a heart attack from seeing him. She has a strong heart."

"You're lying. Why would a superstar want a mediocre, half-witted journalist to write an article about him?"

"Oh, stop putting me down for me doing my job, which I am very passionate about. You've always tried to show me up, ever since we were younger. You're just jealous that I am actually going places and you're not. Get off your high horse, Lyndsay Ana!"

"*Please*! I'm not the one on the high horse here! The golden child acting all high and mighty. I made a few mistakes. So, what? I'm fixing it! At least I have a husband who has been with me since high school. You didn't even have a boyfriend growing up. You were just a natural boy repellent."

"I didn't have time for a relationship. Unlike you, I was studying! And I actually did something for myself by putting myself through college and getting a degree that could get me places."

"And you don't think I'm trying to do something for me and my family? I'm working full time to put my husband through his classes so we can have a better life." Lyndsay Ana shook her head. "You could've at least given us a warning that he was coming. So we could've maybe cleaned up the place? He's a superstar! Who knows what he was thinking when he walked into this farm house."

"Cole was the one who generously offered to help you move back in. You don't know him at all! He has an infectious smile that makes everyone beam with joy. I'm sure he would understand that a normal person's house would be a little messy. He's not stuck up like you may think he is."

Suddenly, the door creaked open. Lyndsay Ana and I looked over to see Cole giving us a wide-eyed look.

"Sorry," he said. "Looking for the bathroom."

"Across the hall," I said, calming down.

Our eyes met for a brief moment as he gave me an apologetic look and shut the door behind him.

"Maybe if you listened before picking fights with me, we could have a better relationship."

Lyndsay Ana straightened herself. "At least I'm married and happy. I'm not single and lonely." She huffed as she raised her nose and pushed past me roughly.

My jaw tightened in anger as I sat down on the bed. I put my head into my hands and continued to breathe deeply. "You just want to pick fights with me over everything," I moaned to myself. Tears came to my eyes as I realized in some ways she was right.

A few minutes later, I heard a knock at the door. "You can come in," I said as I looked at the floor.

"I talked to your sister," Cole said as he sat next to me.

"Oh? What did she say?" I asked softly.

"That she's sorry but she doesn't want to admit that she was wrong," Cole said.

"That's so like her," I whispered. "What did you hear?"

"Everything," he answered simply. "You guys yelled pretty loud. I came to intervene but was too late as it seemed you two were finished." He gave a soft chuckle. "You know, you're more beautiful when you smile."

"How do you know that?" I asked curtly. "What if I have an ugly smile?"

"I don't think a true smile that comes from happiness—from your soul—along with the sparkle in your eyes that everyone sees . . . well, I don't think those kinds of smiles could ever be ugly. I think the most beautiful things about those smiles is that they show you're truly happy and you're showing it to everyone. That joy can spread and others can be happy with you. Smiles make the world a better place, and yours is very beautiful, Crystal Ann." Cole placed a warm hand on my shoulder.

A few tears fell down my face. His words were the most beautiful someone ever said to me.

"Hey, show me your face and let me know you are laughing at my cheesy statements," he begged.

I looked up at him, a few more tears falling softly down my cheeks. "Did you get that from a movie you acted in?" I tried to laugh off what he said.

Cole chuckled as he turned his body toward me. "I might have."

"Well, you memorized that part really well if it is from a movie."

"I'm glad you agree." He winked. He gently wiped the tears from my face. "We came here to help your sister move back in. Don't you think we should help sometime?"

"Yeah. You're right," I said, rising. "Let's do this then."

Chapter Seven

The orange-red hues of the sunset filled the sunroom with beautiful colors. The paint and the sunset mixed together on the walls, creating a picture of fire dancing. As I sat on the sofa relaxing, I closed my eyes and took in the warmth of the setting sun and the colors of the sunset on my eyelids. Peace came to my heart as I began to drift into sleep.

Someone sat next to me, and I collapsed into the chest of a man. "Papa?" I asked as my eyes opened, but it wasn't him. Cole gave me a smile as he looked down at me.

"You look funny when you sleep." He grinned.

"Sleep isn't meant to look pretty," I commented softly as I sat up straight.

Just as Cole was about to reply, a call came in on his phone. He glanced at his phone and sighed. His grin disappeared as his eyes become cold.

"Excuse me just a moment." Cole answered the phone and went out the back door onto the patio.

The sunset faded into the dark purple of night and the full moon rose.

"You'll be gone soon," I said to the moon. "Soon you'll be covered with clouds, and no one will see you or your friends, the stars, through the winter months. No gazing upon your beauty in the middle of a clear and humid night, though your beauty does come from the sun shining upon you in its glory."

I heard my mother give a soft chuckle, distracting me from my train of thought.

"Saying such odd things. You have always done that, ever since you were young," Mom said. "Cherry pie?" She held a small plate of pie.

"No, I'm all right. I had some earlier."

"Then why don't you give it to Cole? He seems like he needs it right now," she said softly.

"Really?" I peeked out of the sunroom windows. I saw Cole's frustrated face as he stood on the terrace. "I'll take it to him, then." I held out my hand to take the plate. I slid open the sliding doors.

"Another movie already?" he asked. "I was just in one. It's always so nonstop. I need a break!" He tapped his foot impatiently. "Why can't I relax too? I have been making movies constantly for the past two years, and I need at least a month more of a break! A few days just isn't enough right now." Cole pinched the bridge of his nose, trying to hold in his frustration before he finally sighed. "Fine. I'll do it."

Cole's eyes met mine as he finally noticed me with his plate of the cherry pie. I motioned to a patio chair for him to sit down across from me. He looked a bit embarrassed as I set down the cherry pie. He gave me a soft smile.

"I hate it when you talk my ear off, Rachel," Cole sighed. "I'll come back to California the day after tomorrow."

My heart sank. *I am starting to like Cole. His serious demeanor gives me chills and makes me blush.* I turned away in my chair as he continued to speak on the phone.

"I'll see you later, Rachel." He hung up his phone. I felt his eyes look at me. "Sorry you had to hear some of that."

"It's no matter. You're a busy superstar. That's your job," I said as the moonlight shined down on us without the interference of city street lights. "I'm sure that whatever movie you're going to be in will be awesome."

The blueness of Cole's eyes pierced as they looked through me. "I was having so much fun here too." He shook his head in disappointment. "I was enjoying your company."

"Why's that?" I asked.

"I like you a lot, Crystal Ann. You're hard-headed, strong-willed, light-hearted," he said with a little chuckle as he took a bite of pie, "and you dealt with having to work with me for this article."

"When does the filming begin?"

105

"Next week." He shook his head.

"Why do you have to go back now?"

"To prepare for the premiere of a movie I was working on a little while ago. We almost had to push back the deadline, but we luckily made it," Cole said.

A small breeze blew as we sat silently while Cole finished his pie. I really didn't know what to say.

"Does this mean I can't complete the article, and you're giving up my story?" I was apprehensive.

"Hmm, you can interview me tomorrow if that's what you'd like," he said. Suddenly, his face lit up with an epiphany. "No! Wait! I can escort you to the movie premiere. You can come to California with me. To see what I *really* do as a superstar!"

"I don't think that is within my budget."

"I'll pay for it," Cole said in a serious tone.

"Wouldn't you feel uncomfortable with me?" I asked.

"Oh, no, Crystal Ann," Cole said with his big, goofy grin. "I told you before that I liked you and want to spend time with you. C'mon! Come to California with me!" he said, almost begging. His puppy eyes made my heart go for a spin.

I shook my head in disbelief. "If I don't get my story tomorrow, then I will have no choice but to follow you to get it. I can't let my boss down."

Cole grinned. "If that's how you want to play," he said as he leaned back in his chair.

Mom knocked on the glass, and we both looked back at her. She opened the sliding door a little bit more.

"Shall I prepare something on the floor for you two?" she asked. "Rhett and Lyzie's room is filled with boxes so they're taking the guest bedroom."

"I don't know if Cole would want to sleep on the floor, Mom," I said.

"I'd love to stay the night as long as you make sweet eggs in the morning. Those are my favorite!" Cole teased.

"Oh? Those are your favorite too? Crys always asked for sweet eggs in the morning. She loves sweet eggs."

I sighed as I shook my head; a small smile of my own gently rested on my lips. "Well, if Cole wants to sleep over, that's fine."

"Yes!" Cole cheered as he celebrated his victory.

*

We both rested on the couches on the other side of the living room. I was having a hard time falling asleep. The moon was shining down brightly on me, but Cole was softly snoring away as he laid on his back. He looked like he was doing yoga, bent in different positions.

I snickered to myself as I stared at his peaceful sleeping self. He looked so cute when he slept. *Too bad he's a devil when he's awake.*

I pushed my warm blanket off as I stood up. A cold chill surrounded me as I walked into the kitchen. The hardwood floor was holding the chill, unlike the shaggy carpet in the living room. I shivered as my bare feet touched the floor of the kitchen.

I walked over to the bar where the few containers of sugar, flour, and other simple ingredients for cooking were kept. I grabbed a medium-sized container and opened it to reveal untouched hot chocolate mix.

"Oh, Mom. You know me all too well," I whispered to myself.

I grabbed the teakettle from the pantry and began to boil some water. *I hope Cole is a deep sleeper. This is the only way I will drink my hot cocoa.*

I sat down at the table as I waited for the teakettle to hiss. Everybody else was behind closed doors on the other side of the house, so I was not concerned about waking them up.

The clock on the stove said 1:28 a.m. I closed my eyes to rest them for a moment, when I heard the squeak of the back sliding door. My eyes shot open in disbelief.

"Cole," I whispered. I quietly got up and wandered over to the entrance of the living room, hiding myself behind the wall as I peeked over. I saw a dark figure standing over Cole. I gasped in horror. "Oh, no, Cole!" I softly cried. I saw the man bring out a knife. "No!" I shouted. The hooded figure looked toward me, his eyes glowing a menacing red. "Leave him alone!" I yelled. I suddenly appeared in front of the hooded figure with a light shooting from my hands.

"You're too late, Crystal Ann," the figure said, unaffected by my light beam. *Light beam?*

"What do you mean?" Tears began to form in my eyes. I looked over and saw Cole had been murdered, his beautiful eyes null of life. "Cole!" I screamed in horror. Then, everything went black.

"Crystal Ann!" Cole said, jolting me awake. I woke up in the chair at the table. The teakettle was hissing for someone to turn it off. "Are you all right?" He held my shoulders.

I didn't speak as I breathed heavily. Tears fell down my face. He gave me a strong and concerned look as he rushed over to the stove, taking the teakettle off the burner. I watched him in amazement. *He's alive.* I looked at the clock and read 1:37. I had fallen asleep for a couple of minutes.

Cole gently helped me up to my feet. Everything felt numb as I fell back into my seat.

"Crystal Ann," he whispered as he gently touched my face. "What's wrong?"

"You died," I whimpered as my lip began to tremble. "Blood was everywhere and you died. Then I died."

"I'm right here, see? I didn't die," he said, holding my hand. I felt him, but it was like he was still a ghost. My hands were so cold, especially compared to his.

"But you died," I sobbed quietly as he put his hands to my face, then wrapped his arms around me while I cried. He didn't say a word as he rubbed my back, and we swayed back and forth.

"What's going on?" Lyndsay stood in the doorway.

The overhead light turned on. "Crystal Ann had a bad dream, it seems," Cole said.

"Oh," Lyndsay said. "That's really nothing to worry about. She has nightmares all the time."

I grabbed Cole's shirt in anger. The bright kitchen light burned my bloodshot eyes. I could hardly breathe, my nose clogged from crying.

"She used to flip out like this when we were children too. It's really nothing to be upset about," she said.

"Oh, all right," he said. "I guess you can go back to bed since it doesn't bother you. I am worried about her, but because you're not concerned, you can go back to sleep. I'll take care of her."

Lyndsay Ana rolled her eyes. She left, leaving the kitchen light on.

"How inconsiderate of her," Cole whispered.

I didn't comment as I slowly let go of his shirt.

"I thought of something funny," he said suddenly.

"What is that?" I asked.

"Your dream. It's funny."

"How is that?" I whispered, squinting at the light.

"You're afraid that I'll leave," he said. "But, remember, Crystal Ann, you're coming with me to finish the job. Now, here comes the funny part. It's like I'm a dog on a leash, and you're the owner trying to teach me tricks."

"How is that funny?" I felt a smile come to my face.

"Because you're my master, and I'll obey you at your every command," he said.

I gently shoved him. "You're an idiot," I taunted.

"Anything my master says must be true." He let go of me and began to shake his butt like he had a tail. I couldn't help but giggle, trying to be quiet. My smile widened.

"Would you like some hot cocoa?" I asked.

"If that'll make my master happy."

"Well, a dog can't have chocolate. I guess you can't," I teased.

"Are you trying to get me not to be a dog?" he asked. His face looked playfully annoyed.

I giggled. "Yes. Because you're not a dog. You're a man, and a good one at that."

He gave me a surprised look; his smile faded as his mouth dropped open a little bit.

"I'll make us some hot chocolate then. How much chocolate do you like?" I asked.

"I like a lot of scoops of the cocoa mix."

I put some cocoa mix in before and after I poured the water for both of us, giving Cole more mix than me. I gave him his to stir and drink as I began to stir mine.

"Do you want some marshmallows?"

"Are they the cute small ones that could look like noses for snowmen?" he asked, in an excited voice.

"Hmm," I said as I opened a cupboard. "It seems we do have them."

"Then I'd like some, please." He sat at the counter.

I put marshmallows in his drink and handed it to him. He immediately began to drink the hot chocolate.

"You didn't tell me it was mint chocolate."

"It's something that helps calm me down so I can sleep," I said.

"You can't sleep at night?"

"Only sometimes when those bad dreams come." I took in the smell of mint.

"How often do you get those dreams?" Cole asked.

"I don't know," I said, a little flustered, trying to think. "It just happens at random times, I guess."

"I'm sorry," he apologized.

"For what?"

"That you have those sorts of dreams."

I looked down at my hands that held the mug of warm hot chocolate, pondering what he said. "It's nothing to worry about."

"How is that?"

"I'm used to it," I commented softly.

"Well, you don't deserve to be used to it," Cole said.

"That's what a lot of people say, but it's not something that someone can simply take away. You can say those words all day but the dreams won't leave."

"Did something happen to you when you were younger?" His voice was soft.

"Uhm . . ." I stuttered as his question caught me off guard. For a split moment, I saw a foot hanging in air, as if floating. I shook my head slightly, making the image go away. "Well, a lot of things happened when I was little. So, maybe."

Cole nodded as he drank the rest of his hot chocolate. "We should go to sleep," he said, wiping his mouth.

I nodded. He went on to the living room as I finished up. I cleaned our mugs and emptied out the teakettle.

By the time I reached the living room, Cole was fast asleep and the moon was beginning to set. I laid down on the couch and fell fast asleep.

Chapter Eight

"Crystal Ann, would you like some breakfast?" My mother beckoned from the kitchen.

My eyes opened as she walked up to me. I smiled. "What's for breakfast?" I asked as I slowly sat up.

"Sweet eggs as your friend requested. He's already at the table enjoying it. He might eat all the sweet eggs, and there will be none for you."

"I can see him doing that," I said with a laugh.

I sat down next to Cole where my food was already set out. I began to eat *right* as I sat down. I stared blankly off into space as I ate.

"She seems out of it," Cole commented to my mother.

"She's always like that in the morning," Mom reassured Cole.

He laughed. "So, she's a bit of an airhead in the morning?"

"I guess you could say that," my sister said as she came around the corner with her husband.

I blinked and continued to stare off into space as they talked about me. I put my fork down as I stopped eating. I felt Cole looking right at me as I looked out the window.

"You going to eat that?" I did not say anything as I sat there. He sighed.

I blinked a few times, picking up my fork. I began to eat again. I felt so tired.

Suddenly, Lyndsay Ana snapped her fingers in front of my face. "I need to tell you something. It's really important."

I looked up and saw my dad standing by the back door.

"Now, I didn't want to be all dramatic or anything, but Rhett and I are proudly pregnant with not just our first child, but with twins," she said, giddy with excitement.

I was suddenly excited and smiling.

"That's awesome, Lyndsay!" Mom said happily.

Tears came to my father's eyes. "I'm going to be a grandpa of twins!"

"You're going to be an aunt, Crystal Ann," Cole said.

I looked back at him with a satisfied look. "I am, aren't I? That's pretty awesome. Congrats, Lyndsay Ana."

"Thank you, Crystal." My sister looked down at her stomach with a small smile.

"You just better be out of my house by then because I don't think I could handle another baby after you, Lyndsay Ana! Let alone two," my mother teased, but I heard a fair warning in her voice.

Everyone laughed as I smiled. *Can my sister really handle a baby, though? Let alone two! She is the baby of my family and doesn't know what it's like to take care of a child, although her husband can be like one sometimes.*

"So, Cole," I said, suddenly in the swing of things. "We tried to go to the Statue of Liberty yesterday, but didn't. . . Why don't we go today?"

His eyes lit up as he gave me a big grin. "That sounds like a lot of fun."

"It's been awhile since I've been there," Mom commented.

Cole happily invited my family. "You guys should come too! It'd be like one big party."

I chuckled at his enthusiasm.

"I've got animals to tend all day," my father said. "I'll have to take a raincheck, but sweetie, you can go."

"Can I, really?" my mom teased with a laugh. "I really do want to go."

"Mom, when Cole invites you to something, he isn't being sarcastic, he's being truthful and sincere in asking you to come with him," My mouth moved on its own. My left pinkie twitched as I mentally took a step back.

Cole gave me a bit of a shocked expression, but I knew he was pleased because I saw the twinkle in his eyes.

"I am feeling a little sick this morning," Lyndsay Ana said dramatically, trying to draw attention to herself.

I don't know why she always has to make everything about herself. She has to be the center of attention and makes sure she's being taken care of by everyone. Cole saw through that last night after I woke up from my nightmare.

"I'm sorry you're feeling that way, Lindsay Ana but. . . Yeah!" Cole turned to Mom. "Crystal Ann is right! You can really come."

"That's fantastic!" she responded.

"Are you sure you're feeling sick, sweetie?" Rhett asked Lyndsay Ana softly. "I know how much you love to visit the Statue of Liberty."

"I really am feeling sick, and I just don't want to go," she whispered back to her husband.

I sighed to myself as I ate the last few bites of my breakfast.

"Thank you, Mom." I excused myself from the table and cleaned my plate in the sink. I dried it and put it away.

"Thank you, Mom," Cole repeated after me, teasing my mother. He stood up and copied my actions.

"Copycat," I muttered under my breath, playfully.

I felt him smirking up a storm behind me.

"Do you need any help with the chores around the house, Mom?" I asked as I came back into the kitchen.

Cole was right behind me, his chest almost leaning against my back. I felt like his hand should've been on my shoulder or his arms around me. I shook my head slightly, trying to get that image out of my mind. *It will never happen.*

"No, not right now." Mom finished cleaning the last plate. "How about you two wait in the front parlor while I get ready to go visit the Statue, huh?"

"Sounds good," I said as I led Cole to the front living room—what my mom calls the parlor.

As we walked in, everything was overpowered with floral design.

"Woah," he said. "Does your mom like floral print?"

"For the most part," I giggled. I sat in the love seat by myself. "She just loves flowers and how they smell. She almost married a florist, she says, but she knew that Papa was the one for her, even though he was a rancher. She, to this day, still does not like pigs. She finds them utterly gross and disgusting. She even hates the taste of them."

"Really?" Cole asked.

"Yeah. I don't like pork much either. I must get it from her."

"I figured that much," Cole laughed. "You don't even like bacon all the time. You're one crazy woman."

"I try to be," I jeered. "You going to sit down?"

"No. I want to stand right now." He looked around the room, as if seeking a clue.

I nodded as I gave him his space. We continued in silence—a peaceful quietness. The kind where everything was serene and we could simply sit and stare at each other all day . . . *Not that we would. That'd just be weird.*

"I'm ready," Mom exclaimed as she came into the parlor.

"All right," I responded standing up. "Let's go."

Cole and I followed Mom out the door and to her truck.

"My truck is a little crowded because it doesn't have back seats, so I hope you two are comfortable with cuddling," my mother teased.

"Mom!" I rolled my eyes.

Cole laughed as he put his arm around me. "Nothing to worry about," he winked. "She smells nice."

Cole and mom laughed, but I couldn't help but blush a little. She got into the driver's side, and I crawled into the middle of the seat. I turned the radio to a top hits station and leaned back. I slouched slightly as I closed my eyes. Cole moved and put his arm around me again. I looked up at him. He smiled down at me. His eyes told me he was definitely flirting.

"This all right?" he asked. "It's a little tight in here with my fat butt and your fat butt."

"I don't know what you're talking about! I have nice curves, but you're a thick stick," I teased.

"Ha!" Cole said. "At least I'm thick."

I burst out laughing. "I don't know if that is such a good thing!"

Cole's eyes went wide, realizing what he said. "You know what I meant!"

Mom turned up the radio. "Don't wanna hear you two lovebirds," she laughed.

"We're not lovebirds." I tried to speak over the loud music.

"I thought we were," Cole joked as he brought his hand down to my waist. "I mean, I'd like to be."

I blushed as he looked at me with serious eyes, even though his face looked like he was joking. My heart beat faster as we stared into each other's eyes. My left pinkie began to twitch uncontrollably. I grabbed my left hand with my right to stop the twitching.

"You're leaning a little on me, Crystal Ann. Please stop," my mom said.

"Sorry." I moved closer to Cole.

"Just kiss already," Mom said. "I promise I won't look."

"Mom!" I whined as I looked away from Cole. Even though we weren't making eye contact, I could still feel him staring at me. "I'm uncomfortable when you stare at me," I whispered.

"I can't help myself sometimes," he whispered in my ear. Then, he looked away and out his window.

*

"Wow," Cole's eyes sparkled when we parked the truck. He whistled as he saw the Statue of Liberty with his own eyes. "Can we go into the torch of Lady Liberty?" he asked.

"No," I said. "No one can go up there."

"I'll go buy the tickets," Mom said. "Hang tight."

We both nodded as we sat in the back of the truck, looking up at the big statue.

"Can we still go to the crown?" Cole squinted to see if there was anyone up there.

"Yeah, but we need special tickets for that."

"Then what is your mom getting tickets for?"

"The ferry."

"Oh, that makes sense," Cole said.

"I'm sorry you won't be able to go up to the crown," I said apologetically.

"I'll bet I can do something. I am not a normal person." He winked.

I shook my head. I had forgotten. *I see him more as a friend than a superstar.*

"I'm sorry."

"No. It's nice that you see me as an equal instead of some god." He gave me a happy smile.

Nearby, I saw a few girls talking among themselves. They were giggling as they made their way up to the truck.

"Cole," I whispered. "Five o'clock." He looked back and saw the small group of girls.

"Shall we run?" he asked with a grin on his face as his eyes met mine.

"What about my mother?"

"The line is probably long. Let's run," He was suddenly up, jumping from the truck.

Shocked, I froze for a moment. "Hey, this isn't a movie, ya know!" I said, trying to stand up. He ran to the other side of the truck and picked me up with ease. I yelped as he grabbed me. He helped me to my feet and we began to run. I laughed as I ran after him. *It's almost like we're in an action movie. Running away from the villains . . . teenage girls!*

I began to lag behind as the girls stopped pursuit when we ran. "Cole!" I was coughing from laughing and running so hard. I stopped, trying to catch my breath. I bent over, placing my hands onto my slightly bent knees, trying to breathe.

"We haven't run far enough yet," he said. "We need to find somewhere to hide." He took my hand and tried to drag me along.

"No, Cole, my side hurts. I can't run anymore," I breathed heavily, trying not to laugh.

"I'll carry you then," he said. "But I am not going to run."

"They stopped chasing us," I wheezed.

He just laughed. "What about the shadow people that are after the princess?"

"What princess?" I asked.

"You, Princess Crystal Ann. The shadows are after my lovely princess," he said, acting like we were in a fantasy world.

"So, now this is a game?" I laughed as I stood up straight, still recovering. Drops of sweat ran down my face.

"No, m'lady. Running from the shadows isn't a game." He winked as he let me get onto his back, and we continued to run away.

Cole gently put me down behind the bathroom building where we could see the Statue of Liberty from a different angle. Cole breathed heavily as he sat down next to me in the shade.

"Wow. You're lighter than most girls but after a while, you get heavy," he laughed.

"I am a little fat," I teased. He casually put his arm around my shoulder again, trying to bring me closer.

"You're not even a little fat. You're the perfect size for your height," he said with a serious face. "Please, don't even tease that you're fat."

"All right," I sighed, rolling my eyes.

He took his arm back as he sat against the back of the building.

"Are the shadows gone?" I played along.

"Let me see," he said in a quiet tone as he got up and peeked around the corner. I stood up and followed him. When I went to look, he suddenly turned around and put his arms over me as I put my back to the building. "The shadows are passing," he whispered as he moved closer. "We must stay quiet. Don't even breathe."

I went to speak, but he gently put a finger to my lips as we waited in silence for several minutes. As I looked up at Cole, I realized that I felt like such a child, running around playing games. It felt nice. As he peered around the corner, my heart began to race. I tried to examine his face to see if he was done. His jaw looked sharp enough to cut as he looked back at me over his shoulder. I felt a chill go up my back as I rubbed my arms, trying to make the goosebumps go away. I felt my left pinkie twitch for a moment as I saw a glimmer of red between our hands.

"The coast is clear." He beckoned me to follow him. "We must get back to headquarters before the boss returns." He began to walk off.

I laughed softly, tears in my eyes, still trying to catch my breath. "I love you, Cole Dakota," I whispered. *And yet you tease my heart like this.* My heart hurt as I bowed my head.

I don't even know if you love me back because you tease me so much.

I followed after him, trying to gain composure as I forced the tears away.

We soon got back to the truck. I smacked my lips together as I hopped into the back after Cole. "I am thirsty from all that running."

"Well, it's too late now. We're back at H.Q., and it seems boss is returning," Cole grinned.

Smiling, my mom appeared, holding a ticket for the three of us for the ferry. "You two look tired. Did you run around?"

"Yes, we did," Cole said, in a serious voice. "The shadows were chasing us."

"Cole." I shook my head.

"Oh? The shadows?" Mom questioned curiously.

"It was nothing." I attempted to sidestep the conversation.

"No, really!" Cole said in a teasing little boy voice. "The shadows chased us, and we had to run away and come back before you came back to make sure you didn't get taken by them."

My mom and I made eye contact as she giggled. "For a man in his twenties, you sure have a child's imagination."

"Same with Walt Disney!" Cole retorted. "What is a world without imagination? Without creativity and art?"

"I guess a dull world," Mom said softly, realizing what Cole was saying. "I guess you're right, but that doesn't mean that you still aren't a man-child."

"I think so too . . . and thanks. I'm proud to be a man-child." Cole nodded, full-on joking. "Let's go, Crystal Ann! Let's go on the ferry."

"It leaves in ten minutes. We need to hurry," Mom said.

We walked quickly to the bay to wait for the ferry to arrive. The ferry was busy as usual. It travels across the water everyday— all day. *Driving the ferry seems like it'd be a boring job.*

The ferry arrived and people began to exit. Several people stared at Cole, trying to identify him, but by the time they figured out who he was, they had been swept away by the unknowing crowd. Cole couldn't help but laugh at their surprised faces.

As soon as we boarded the ferry, people immediately began to approach him. He looked a little uncomfortable as people started asking him personal questions and asking for his autograph on spare paper.

He had nowhere to escape except into a small bathroom. I walked up to a tourist and asked if I could have his hat.

I explained to him my poor grandmother was getting too hot and needed some shade, but her hat flew off while we took off into the bay. I offered to buy it from him, and the tourist was hesitant at first. But, he let me buy his hat for forty bucks. *Yeah . . . forty bucks. A little pricey for a used hat. Whatever. I'll just tell Cole to pay me back.*

I walked over to the bathroom and knocked on the door. "Cole, it's Crystal Ann. I have a present that you need to pay me back for," I sang through the slab of wood separating us.

"What kind of present?" he asked.

"You have to open it to see."

The door unlocked and slowly opened. His hand came out and grabbed my hand, gingerly pulling me into the bathroom. I stumbled into the cramped restroom, and he closed the door, locking it. He breathed out heavily with relief. The bathroom was small. We weren't cramped in such a way that we couldn't move in the bathroom, but we would still have to stumble around a little bit to get out.

"Here," I said, handing him the hat.

"A hand-me-down hat?"

"You seem ungrateful," I commented, with a bit of sass. "I'll just take it, and you can be bombarded with crowds wanting your autograph."

"I'll have it."

"Fifty bucks, buddy," I offered as I held out my hand.

"How about a kiss?"

"Ha!" I laughed. "No. Fifty bucks." I motioned with my hand for him to give me the money.

"No, thanks," he said.

"Pfft," I teased as I put the hat on him. "Fine then. Fifty bucks might have bought you a kiss, but not anymore."

"Oh, darn," he chuckled. He put on the hat and pulled the bill down over his face so that no one would recognize him unless they looked really hard. "I am taking you to California."

"I thought you were kidding," I said softly.

"Well, maybe that can be your fifty bucks."

"How is that fifty bucks? That's too much." I tried to squeeze past him to get out the door.

"Crystal Ann," Cole said seriously. "I want you to be one of the first to see my new movie coming out."

"I can watch it in theaters opening night." I shrugged.

"Crystal Ann," he said softly. His eyes turned serious as he looked at me. "I won't give you your story."

"That seems unfair. You asked for me to do the story in the first place."

"Just come."

"It seems unreasonable. I can just sit down with you and ask my questions." I shrugged again. "I'll meet you outside."

He put his hand on the doorknob. "No. Not until you say yes." He was teasing but also serious.

I rolled my eyes. "Then I say yes."

"Pinkie promise. I am also telling your mother so you have to come," he said.

"You're acting like a child," I scoffed.

"To get what I want I have to sometimes."

"Okay," I whispered. We pinkie promised. I saw the red thread appear for a moment as our pinkies intertwined. He let me out. "Come out when you're ready."

The people who were watching the bathroom for Cole to come out were surprised to see me. I gave them a kind smile as I walked back over to Mom. The ferry approached the statue.

"It's so much smaller than I remember," I commented.

"It's because you were so much smaller when we last came here." She laughed.

"You're right."

Cole came out of the bathroom and walked up behind us.

"How was your bathroom break?" I asked.

"Great," he teased. "Hey, Crystal Ann is coming with me to California tomorrow."

"Uhm," I began as I looked at my mom. "I—"

"She agreed to it, too, with a pinkie promise." He grinned.

You're an evil man, Cole Dakota.

"Oh, wow," Mom said, giving me a worried look. "When will you be returning?"

"Probably next Sunday. That's when you have to go back to work. Right, Crystal Ann?" he asked.

"Uh, yeah." I breathed out. "I just don't think I should go."

"Why not?" Cole quickly asked. "You showed me around New York; now it's my turn to show you around Los Angeles."

"That sounds like fun," Mom said. "I wish I could go."

"You could if you wanted to," Cole said.

"I have to tend to the farm, but thanks anyways."

Cole couldn't help but smile. He turned to me. "Please, let me show you around Los Angeles. You haven't been, right?"

"No, I haven't been." I shook my head. "Too busy working on the farm when I was little. Couldn't really leave on vacation too often."

"Then, please." Cole said, begging.

"You should go, Crystal Ann," Mom chimed in. "I think it's a good opportunity to have him take you to Disneyland." Then, she winked.

"You've never been to Disneyland?" Cole gasped.

I couldn't help but laugh at his cute face. "No, but I don't feel like I need to."

"I am taking you there. I am kidnapping you and taking you to Disneyland," Cole said.

"As long as we have our interview," I said.

"Fine with me."

"You've said that before," I observed. "I think we need to write it in blood."

We all laughed as the ferry stopped and let us off. Other people filed in as the ferry got ready to leave again.

"Wow, her feet are so big," Cole laughed, looking at the statue's feet. "Every time we've filmed in New York, I have never have the chance to come close like this."

"Really?" I asked.

"Yeah, and if I did have to film with the statue, it'd be with a green or blue screen," he sighed. "It's expensive to rent the island for shooting."

"Oh, I'll bet it is."

We continued walking toward the building. I couldn't help but look up in awe at the statue made so long ago. *It is hard to believe that it is still in almost perfect condition. Although, because it is plated in copper it slowly turned green over time. It's still amazing and beautiful.*

"It's so much more amazing up close," Cole commented in awe. I saw the sparkle in his eyes as he looked up. "I should update my Twitter and Facebook." He pulled out his phone and lifted up his hat to expose his face to the camera. "Join me, Crystal Ann." He put his arm around me, dragging me into the shot.

He snapped a few pictures of me smiling as I'm looking at him. *A few of the shots probably caught me blushing as well.*

"C'mon, Crystal Ann, look at the camera." He started to take another picture.

Hesitantly, I looked at the camera and tried to smile.

"You're not smiling like you were before."

"Because that was natural," I said.

He snapped a picture of us both and quickly pulled away.

"Just delete them. I probably look bad." I begged, trying to get his phone from his hand.

"Too late. I already posted them." Cole laughed as he put his phone away in his pocket before I could reach it.

"Why?"

"Because I am sure my fans would love to meet you." Cole smiled as he walked over to the building and touched it. I followed behind him as I yanked his hat down in front of his eyes.

"Hey!"

"That's for posting pictures of me with you," I said with sass.

Cole scoffed at me as he pulled his hat up to where it was before.

We spent a half an hour at the base before Cole was ready to go into the statue.

"We need reserved tickets for that," I insisted.

"Come with me," he said as he took my hand.

I was surprised, though I knew I shouldn't be. My pinkie twitched as he dragged me toward the entrance. It stopped twitching after a few moments of him holding my hand, but it felt like it would never stop.

We walked up to the guard. "I'm sorry, sir, I don't have a ticket to go up to the crown, but I'd like to."

"Sorry, kid, can't go past," the guard said.

Cole took off his hat. "Please, I'll do anything. My girlfriend and I would like to go up."

I felt my cheeks grow hot as my jaw dropped. I went to speak but stopped before I uttered a peep.

"Oh, sweetie, it's okay. I think he should know who I am." Cole winked as he kissed my cheek.

I squealed in my mind as he kissed my cheek. He gently squeezed my hand. My left pinkie began to twitch again, but luckily, Cole was holding my right hand. I shoved my left hand into my back pocket. In my mind, I asked it to stop and it did.

"Oh, wow! You're Cole Dakota!" the guard said. "My whole family loves your movies."

"I'm glad they do," Cole said. He pulled me closer.

"We had no idea you had a girlfriend," the guard said as he smiled at me. He seemed amazed that Cole was running around with a normal girl—me.

"It was a recent thing. I love her with all my heart," he said. He leaned into the guard's ear and whispered something. I couldn't quite hear or understand what he said.

"Oh, whoa. When?" the guard asked.

"What?" I asked aloud, but I was ignored by them both.

"Probably within the next few months. Do you follow my Tweets?" Cole asked.

"My daughter does."

"Then you'll know soon enough."

"What?" I asked again, out loud, with a little more volume.

"I think you'll find out sometime." The guard winked. He chuckled, as if suddenly his day seemed brighter.

"Could we maybe go past? I'll pay your organization the amount of money that would go toward purchasing a reserved ticket in the first place." Cole gave the guard a grin.

"A few autographs on my notepad, and I'll let you pass. But just this once," the guard said with a happy smile. "And don't tell anyone that I let you pass either."

"What about my mom?" I asked on the way up to the crown.

"She didn't want to go up to the crown with us," Cole said.

"You had this planned out?"

"Yeah, pretty much."

It took several minutes to get up to the crown. We sat in peaceful silence as we journeyed up. When we arrived, I couldn't help but smile and gawk at the view.

"Wow," I said as I looked out over the city, holding onto the railing. "Man, this is scary."

"Are you afraid of heights like your mom?" he asked.

"Yeah. I am shaking. The view, though. My mom told me she was scared of heights, too, and brought me up here when I was younger. She told us that this statue would represent the time we overcame one of our greatest fears. Even though it's still pretty terrifying."

His face was fearless as he looked out from the crown. "That's pretty amazing, Crystal Ann. I remember when I became a full-time actor, I had to get over my fear of heights. I had to deal with high places all the time. So, I've become immune," he explained as he looked at me. "You really are scared, aren't you?"

"Oh, yeah, why do you ask?"

"Your knuckles are white," Cole said. "You didn't have to come up here if you didn't want to."

"Yes, I did because I have to continue to face my fears." I laughed, shaking my head. "But, as long as someone doesn't threaten to push me or touch me in a way that would seem like they're going to push me off, I'll be good."

"It's beautiful. Thank you for bringing me here, Crystal Ann," Cole said sincerely.

"You're welcome," I said softly. "Let's head back."

"Yeah. The moment is over."

Chapter Nine

I watched as Mom drove away in her truck. I gave a small wave as she disappeared into the ongoing traffic.

"You really love your family, huh?" Cole asked. I turned toward him as he smiled at me.

"Yeah. I really do love them," I stated. "Shall I help you pack?"

"Why? I could have the hotel do that." Cole shrugged.

"Wouldn't you want them to have an easy job today?" I tried to hint.

Cole's eyebrows rose in surprise. "Yes. But, you need to pack too, don't you?"

My smile disappeared.

"You promised," Cole warned.

"I know."

"You don't have to keep the promise if you don't want to." His smile was gone.

I didn't say anything for a moment. "It's just that, I don't know you very well," I said suddenly.

Cole gave me a sad look. "I won't make you do anything you don't want to."

"Going to California for my job, though?"

"Don't some reporters go to the site of the disaster to report the story?" Cole questioned. "It's not like you're going to someplace where a volcano erupted or an earthquake has happened."

"I know, but this isn't a disaster," I spoke through clenched teeth.

"It would be a disaster if you don't go," he whispered to me. His eyes filled with a sincere desire for me to come with him.

I couldn't help but blush as I turned away. "Oh, stop trying to flatter me."

"You like to be flattered, though," Cole teased. "You love to blush. You love it when I give you my attention."

I went all the more red because he was right. *I do like his attention.* I crossed my arms over my chest and tried to look away.

"Look at me, Crystal Ann," he said. "C'mon, you know you wanna look at me. You want to stare into my beautiful eyes of blue."

I grabbed my shirt tighter under my arms, hopefully unnoticed.

Cole laughed as he tried to look at my face, but I turned away like a small child.

"Is this a game?" Cole asked, playfully.

I shook my head. *I'm so embarrassed.*

Cole gently touched my chin with his hand. He looked intensely into my eyes with a serious face.

"I want to fall in love with you over and over again, Crystal Ann," Cole admitted to me. "I want my red thread of fate to connect with your pinkie. I feel like it does, at least," Cole whispered more to himself as he looked away momentarily. "I wish I didn't have to leave until the end of two weeks because I know I could make you fall in love with me by then, but I need you to come with me to California."

"Why are you saying this to me?" I pulled away slightly. This was getting too weird for me.

Cole took his hand back. "I may not look like it, but I am a romantic kind of guy. I'd sit with you as you watch chick flicks and cry with you when Marley dies in the end of *Marley & Me*."

"I . . . I don't understand," I said, stumbling over my words.

"Crystal Ann, I fell madly in love with you after we first met—you were independent and you saw me as a person. I have wanted that so badly in someone. All everyone ever sees is a god-like person whom they wish to worship. But you, Crystal Ann, you see me as a regular person. I don't blame you because I made you spill your iced tea, but still. I love how sassy you are. I love how you hold yourself as you walk and how you talk. I love you, Crystal Ann, and I want you to love me. Please come with me."

I was stunned speechless. My legs felt faint. "Cole, I . . ." I began.

"I know you don't love me, yet," Cole said. "But I want you to. I am so selfish I'd drag you across the country for you to fall in love with me."

Tears came to my eyes. "I'm scared," I whispered. Tears began to storm my face. I backed up.

"Why?" he asked.

"I'm scared you're lying to me," I whispered truthfully, continuing to keep my distance. We both stood still.

"You're just going to have to trust me, then," Cole said.

I let him come close as he took my hand with one of his. The other came to my face and gingerly wiped away some tears. "Please, come with me," he begged.

"I like it better when you're not so serious with me." I looked away.

"I can arrange that," he said kindly.

"Oh, just . . . I'll go." A relieved sigh washed over me. "But, only because you want me to, and I still need your interview."

"Don't cry, again, please," he laughed.

"Does it scare you?"

"It made me feel like a monster," Cole said truthfully.

"I'll try not to cry again." I chuckled and cleared my throat. My eyes continued to gaze at the concrete. *I'm not sure I can look up at him for maybe a few more hours. I feel so awkward now. I wonder if Cole feels the same way. He was so serious; it was scaring me. I have to trust that he is serious, but, it still scares me that someone could like — no — love me.*

"You can cry, just make sure it's for a good reason."

"All right," I laughed it off.

"Do you want to help me pack, then I'll help you pack?" he asked.

"Perv, I'll pack myself. And what about the hotel staff packing your bags for you?"

"Ha! Perv? I'm going to be seeing your whole closet someday if my plans work out."

I blushed.

"You look surprised." Cole flashed a grin at me as our eyes locked on one another.

"You're very confident." I couldn't help but grin back at him.

"I hope to be," Cole smiled. "I really do want to be right."

"Just shush," I said. "I'll go pack."

"I don't have your number. I need to make sure you don't run away."

"Here." I offered, handing him my phone. "Hold onto it. I'll surely come back for my phone."

"No. I want something that you can't replace," Cole said. He saw my bracelet. "Let me hold onto that."

My uncle had made the bracelet for me before he died. I hesitated because the bracelet hadn't left my wrist in years.

"I see that it holds a lot of value to you. I promise I won't chuck it across the street once I have it in my possession."

"That makes me not want to give it to you." I took it off slowly and gave it to Cole. "Here you go."

"And your phone?" he asked.

"I thought you wanted my bracelet instead."

"And your phone. I want your phone," he cooed.

"Fine." I handed him my phone, and to my surprise, he handed me his phone. "What?"

"Just hold onto it. I know the number to my phone. I'll call you if I need you sooner than we're planning." he said.

I grinned. "All right," I said as I slipped his phone into my pocket.

"Are you going to sell my phone on eBay?" he asked.

I was a bit surprised he remembered that conversation. "Yeah. I just might. Sell all your contacts for a thousand bucks each."

We laughed and continued to walk down the street as the sun burned bright in the sky.

*

I walked into my apartment. The three o'clock sun was shining on my bed through my window. I threw my keys into a big seashell I found on the beach one day, now serving as a kitchen table decoration.

"Where's my suitcase? Oh! Yes, of course," I said as I ran over to my bed. I tossed clothes that I had stuck under there (because I didn't feel like cleaning) and scattered them all over the floor. I grabbed my suitcase and opened it. I ran to my dresser. There weren't a lot of clean clothes. I moaned as I grabbed what I could from my drawers and threw them into my suitcase.

I ran to the dirty clothes on the floor. I began to smell them to see if they at least smelled clean. *Maybe I'll sneak in a few loads at Cole's house. Wouldn't he love that?*

"Ew!" I gagged as I threw a shirt behind me. I continued to sort by smell before closing my suitcase. With a sigh of relief, I was done packing. I picked up all the clothes and threw them back under my bed, trying to make my apartment look nice again.

I looked around. I went over to my oven to make sure it was off. *Although, I'm sure the apartment would've exploded by now if it were on.* I made sure nothing was plugged in and that I had my keys.

Just as I checked my butt pocket, Cole's cell phone rang. I walked away from my kitchen with a calm expression. "Hello?"

"Are you ready for your adventure?"

"If you call running away for two weeks an adventure, sure," I teased.

"Great. Now, what's your address?" Cole asked. I could hear that he was in a car.

"Oh, I can just meet you somewhere," I offered as I grabbed my suitcase from my bed and walked toward the door. I felt as if I was forgetting something.

"It's no trouble," he said.

"But . . ."

"It's not like I'm going to stalk you. We're friends at least, aren't we? C'mon," he insisted.

I rolled my eyes as I told him. I opened the door and walked out as my landlord was standing there.

"Crystal Ann," he said, surprised.

"Hello, Roger."

"Where are you off to?"

"The airport. I need to hurry," I said, trying to push past.

"Why is that?" he asked.

"For my job. Please." I tried to cut him short. "I need to go."

Cole was silent on the phone.

"Can you at least pay me this month's rent, right now?" he asked.

"Oh, yes. I almost forgot!" I said as I put the suitcase down to my side. I slipped the phone into my left front pocket. I reached for my wallet from another pocket but it wasn't in that pocket. I rushed back inside my room. I scanned the room quickly as I looked under my covers. The landlord came in at his pleasure and looked around at my organized mess.

"I love what you've done with the place," he said sarcastically.

I sighed to myself as I rolled my eyes and opened my desk drawers. I slid them open and saw that my wallet was on the top of the desk. I groaned as I stood up. *This is just . . . stupid.*

I took out the money and handed it over to Roger. "Need anything else?" I asked as I put my wallet into my back pocket.

"Should be about it." Roger said, counting the money with a small nod. "See you later, Crystal Ann."

I ran out of my apartment, grabbing the phone from my pocket. "Sorry, my landlord is kind of pushy," I said when I was outside.

"I heard that, kid!" Roger said from down the hall. I couldn't help but chuckle.

"It's all right," Cole said. I somehow knew he was smiling at me. "We're almost there. The plane leaves pretty soon."

"How soon?" I asked as anxiety began to take over. I rushed down the stairs.

"Like, in an hour and a half," he said.

"Are we gonna make it past security by then?" I was worried. As I said that, I missed a step. I squealed as I fell onto my back. My suitcase fell on my face, and the phone went flying. I heard it land as I moaned and groaned.

"Crystal Ann, you clumsy-ass, get out of my way," I heard a familiar voice hiss.

I growled as I got up quickly. "You shouldn't call people names, Patrick," I said as I grabbed my suitcase.

"Your nose is bleeding," he casually said as he pushed past and walked up the stairs.

"Pfft," I scoffed as I felt the blood dripping. I grabbed the banister as I hurried down the stairs. I picked up the phone. It had a few scratches on it. I hissed at myself at the pain I caused the poor, unsuspecting phone. I picked it up. "Hello?"

"Crystal Ann? Are you okay?" I could envision him standing up in concern, but I knew he was in a car.

"Yeah. I always . . . Uh . . . Yeah I'm just fine," I said as I tried to cover my nose while holding my suitcase and keeping the phone to my ear.

"Well, we're here. Do I need to come in?" Cole asked.

"No. I'm coming out, now." I put the phone into my cleavage. I held my nose to stop the bleeding as I came out of my apartment complex. Cole hung up the phone. He came up to me. Blood dripped down my arm.

"What happened?" he asked.

"I fell down the stairs." I tried to shrug it off with a small smile.

"It's not really funny," he said. "I have tissues in the limo. Get in."

"I need—"

"I'll get it. Just grab the tissues." he said as he grabbed my suitcase from my hand and went to the trunk.

"I got it, Master Dakota," said his driver.

"Thank you," he said as Cole climbed into the limo behind me. I was putting tissues over my nose.

"You're making a really big mess."

"I'm sorry," I tried to apologize.

"I meant of yourself. I don't care about the limo. I don't want you to look like you got attacked by some gang," he said, his face serious.

I couldn't help but smile behind all the tissues.

"Here, give me your arm. I'll help you wipe it off." he said.

"Would you like some water, Master Dakota?" asked the driver. He looked back from the driver seat, waiting for an open spot to start driving on the road.

"Is there some in here?" Cole questioned as he looked around, only seeing liquor.

"Yes. In the cabinet. Please, grab some for your friend," the driver said politely.

"Thank you," Cole said. He opened up the cabinet and found a few water bottles. At this, the driver rolled up the window that divided us. "This'll have to do, I suppose," he said. He grabbed a few tissues, put some water onto them, and helped clean off my arm as I held the other tissues to my bleeding nose.

"Thanks."

"Don't be flirting with me now," he laughed as a smile crept onto his face.

I scoffed slightly as he finished up.

"We'll change your shirt in the airport. I'll get you one that has Snoopy and says 'I ♥ NY,'" Cole smiled.

I looked at Cole and shook my head. "You're just being funny." I leaned back in the seat.

Cole switched seats, so he was facing me. "Lie down," he said, ignoring my comment. "It'll help the bleeding stop faster."

I gave a nod as my smile faded. I laid down and closed my eyes as I held the tissues to my nose. *These tissues are making it hard to breathe. Or is it my heart that is making it hard to breathe?*

*

My clogged nose stopped bleeding as we approached the airport. Cole and I got out of the limo, and the driver insisted on putting the bags on a trolley. I stretched my legs as I offered to help push the cart in, but Cole quickly took over as he thanked the driver and we walked into the airport.

"So, what plane are we on?" I asked.

"My private jet," he said with a smile.

My eyes widened. "A—A private jet?" I asked.

Cole chuckled. "C'mon, let's hurry," he said as he motioned me to follow.

He is a superstar and all, but it's hard to believe that he has a private jet. Does he make that much money? Like, holy cow.

This is amazing. I am also nervous. He said such wonderful things to me, and it scares me a little bit that he wanted to get to know me, personally. He wasn't lying or else he wouldn't have dragged me out this far. I'm so afraid I'm going to be rejected in the end. Cole wouldn't do that, though, would he? Maybe. He said he wanted to get to know me, not the other way around.

Why am I even thinking about this? I shouldn't worry about it until the time comes. That kind of sounds like I'll be taking advantage of Cole until then. This—Ugh! This is so hard!

"Crystal Ann, are you all right? You seem flustered." Cole brought me out from my daze. We were standing in front of his plane.

"Oh," I softly said. "Yeah, I'm fine."

Cole raised an eyebrow as he looked at me. "You totally sure?" he asked.

I nodded. "Just a big step. I've never been on a plane before," I admitted.

"Have you traveled even a little bit?"

"No. Never even been to California before. Never been outside of New York."

"Wow! That's impressive to me. I'm definitely taking you to Disneyland, and you can't object because your life isn't complete without going there." He helped me onto the plane as some attendants took our bags. I couldn't help but smile. *I think I'm a bit too old for Disneyland.*

"Whoa," I said as I entered the jet. It was smaller than I imagined, but it looked like a lounge instead of the regular interior of planes that I saw in movies.

"Looks expensive, right?" Cole walked past me and sat down near a window, putting his seatbelt on.

"Yeah. All this leather looks expensive," I gawked. "Almost too expensive for me to sit down."

"Well, you're going to fall over from take-off if you don't sit down. Please, take a seat," Cole said. "Nothing is too expensive for you."

I couldn't help myself as I continued to look around.

"Please, we'll be taking off soon. We'd all appreciate if you sat down, ma'am," the captain said as he walked in, greeting us with a smile.

"You're not planning on sitting by me? Sad." Cole said as he put his finger close to his eye and ran his finger down his face like a teardrop.

I giggled. "I'll sit by you, but just once." I walked over and sat down.

"Do you know how to put on a seat belt?" he asked.

"I can figure it out." I grabbed the seatbelt and gave it blank stare for a moment.

Cole's hands went over mine as he gently helped me buckle myself. "Now you know," he said in a warm and low voice.

I felt my cheeks flush as he held my hands for a moment before letting them go.

"You two ready?" asked a perky flight attendant.

"Yes, we are," Cole reassured. "If you will take us to my backyard."

The woman laughed. "Of course, Mr. Dakota," she laughed as she went into the cockpit. She soon came back out.

"Do you know how to fly?" she asked me.

"She doesn't," Cole quickly said.

She kindly explained to me that there were three exits. One in the back, and two in the front. She told me that there was a life jacket underneath my seat, just in case, and life rafts in the ceiling.

After she was done explaining everything, she said we were taking off soon. She gave me a small nod when I told her I understood.

"You excited or scared?" Cole asked.

"I just can't believe I'm doing this," I said as I looked at Cole. "This doesn't seem real."

"Well, it doesn't at first, but once you get into the sky—it's pretty amazing." He smiled.

I didn't mean it that way, Cole. You dummy.

The engines continued to roar louder and louder as the jet's flaps moved up and down.

"Woah," I couldn't help saying as I looked out the window.

"Do you wanna switch spots?" Cole asked.

"Can we?"

"Hurry, or we'll take off into the ceiling," he said. We re-buckled in each other's seats. I watched the wings as the jet began to move.

I started to giggle like a little girl as I looked out the small window. It felt like I was in a car at first as the plane began to move.

"It's okay to be afraid of takeoff. If you need to you can hold my hand," Cole said.

"Oh, all right." I looked back out the window.

The jet slowly started going faster and faster. As the airplane started to accelerate, my heart began to race as excitement seeped in. I began to anticipate the plane tilting up in takeoff, but we suddenly began to slow down. Everything died as we came to a stop. I looked at Cole with a confused look.

"Sorry for the delay," the pilot said over the speaker. "We have a minute before we can take off because another plane is taking off right now. Please wait patiently for takeoff by keeping your seatbelts on."

"Did your excitement die?" Cole seemed to know me so well.

I nodded my head. "Yeah. It was exciting and then. . . Bam! We stopped."

Cole laughed. "It's all right. It'll come back. Just lean a little forward."

I leaned a little forward so my back wasn't touching the back of the chair.

"Now, keep leaning like that as much as you can," he said with a small nod.

"Okay," I said with determination.

After a minute the plane began to move again. We accelerated faster than we had before. I couldn't help but be pushed back into my seat. The smile returned to my face as I felt like I was on a roller coaster. I began to giggle uncontrollably as I felt the jet tilt up.

"Oh my gosh!" I said as I suddenly became a little scared and put my hand onto Cole's chest. My fist clenched his shirt. "This is insane. I feel the G-forces pushing against me!"

Cole laughed as he took my hand in his. He leaned back in his seat, taking a deep breath. He looked a little uncomfortable. Cole gently squeezed my hand as the plane slowly jerked up to the right altitude for several minutes. I couldn't help but laugh even more as the plane jerked.

"I'm glad you are enjoying yourself," Cole said in a whisper. I looked over at him curiously. He didn't seem to be doing well.

"Are you all right?"

"This is just my least favorite part," Cole spoke softly as he looked at me.

"Is it because of *Panic in the Skies?*" I asked.

"So, you have seen me act," he laughed, trying to smile. "But, yeah, partly because of that. I hate takeoff because of that movie. I had to do my own stunts. Every time a plane takes off now I can't help but feel my stomach sink."

"Are you okay with landing?"

"As long as it's not crashing," Cole teased.

I gently squeezed his hand to try and comfort him. I looked out the window once more as we began to soar above the clouds. I couldn't help but gasp at the beauty above the clouds.

Chapter Ten

The sun never seemed to set as we made it to California on the six-hour flight. I felt so tired. It was probably around midnight in New York. For the past few days I'd been asleep by now. It was only nine o'clock in California. The sky was black. Hardly a star shone in the sky, because of light pollution.

"You look tired," Cole teased as he led me to a limo.

"I never knew traveling could be so. . . so tiring." I yawned.

"Well, when we get to my estate, you can rest easy." Cole opened the door for me, letting me in and letting me sit down first before he slid in after me.

"Sure," I teased. "It's a really big house, and I won't be allowed in the west wing because that's your secret place."

"Ha! You're also not a captive. I didn't kidnap you," Cole said with a smile.

"Are you sure? It feels a lot like kidnapping to me," I jested with another yawn.

"If it helps you feel better, you're allowed in my room." He winked.

I scoffed as I smacked his arm playfully. "I'm not gonna go into your room," I answered in a sassy tone as I looked out the window of the limo.

"It's a lot different than New York, isn't it?" Cole asked.

"It's very different. So many palm trees. I've never actually seen palm trees." I looked at the massive trees. They seemed to go a hundred feet into the air.

"They're extremely hard to grow," Cole said.

"They are?"

"Yeah. It—I can't really explain how hard it is, unless you experience it yourself." Cole gave a little nod of defeat.

"I see," I laughed as I looked out the window again. "I didn't think you'd try to grow one."

"What do you mean?" Cole asked.

I gave him a sarcastic look while I looked back over at him. "*You* tried to grow a palm tree, right?"

"Yes."

"I thought you'd have a gardener for that."

"Well, what if I wanted to try to grow one on my own?" He looked at me seriously.

I couldn't help but laugh at his serious expression.

"What?" he questioned, seeming a little annoyed.

"I think it's kind of funny. I mean, you tried to grow a palm tree on your own, and I'm assuming that you didn't even ask a gardener for help. I just find it funny that you tried to do something so hard by yourself without any help."

Cole raised an eyebrow. "You're saying I should've asked for help?"

"If you didn't know how to grow a tree, then, yeah. I think you should've asked for help instead of trying to do it by yourself. It's like a kid that isn't bright at math and doesn't understand the concept of what he's working on. The kid doesn't ask for help because he doesn't understand it and ultimately ends up failing the class. He didn't ask for help because he was ignorant, or maybe he didn't want to understand, but if he listened to the teacher and asked for help and heard out what they would have to say and let them teach him, he could've learned a lot of things and passed the class in the first place instead of failing," I said with a little smile.

"I guess I never thought of it that way."

"Not a lot of people do. I always listened to the teachers and somehow got subject matter the first time."

"Teacher's pet?" Cole teased.

"Oh, of course." I rolled my eyes as we both laughed.

We smiled at each other before we awkwardly looked away. At least, I felt awkward.

"Thank you for coming, Crystal Ann," Cole said.

I gave him a side glance. "You dragged me here," I teased. "Why would you have to thank me for coming?"

"Because, your company has given me comfort. I'd appreciate if you came to my filming," Cole said softly.

"Cole—I—I don't know when they start, but I do have a job to get back to, and you said that a premiere for your movie is close to the end of my two weeks."

"I know, you're right about the movie premiere, which isn't for the movie you saw me shooting in New York, but my next filming does start in a few days, and I had asked to get the—what would you call them—'difficult to handle' parts over with." Cole said. "I'd like you to be there."

"Oh." I felt a little stupid at my confusion.

There was silence between us as I watched the dark landscape.

"I just want to let you know that there are probably going to be paparazzi at my home," Cole said, in a serious voice. "I hid from them really well in New York because we kept the movie under the radar, but my house, sadly, is not. So, they're probably going to take pictures of you, if they can. I mean, they can try, but I'll try and protect you."

I couldn't help but smile as I looked at Cole. "All right. Are they always that pushy?"

"Oh, you have no clue," Cole sighed. "They broke into my house once to try and take a picture of me in the shower."

My eyebrows rose. "Wha—?"

"Yes, it really did happen," Cole said, chuckling. "It's a funny story, really. He didn't know that I was an early riser, and I had already taken my morning shower. He sneaked right past me so I tackled him, breaking his camera in the process, and sued him."

"That's not really funny. I hope you called the cops to arrest him as well."

"Let's just say that no one breaks into my house anymore."

People are so disgusting. They'd break into Cole's house to get nudes of him? Maybe they shouldn't be so brash and just wait for him to pose for a magazine. If he ever would. I just don't know how people can be so disgusting and awful. It's astonishing what people want to see from another person. I feel sick to my stomach.

"Wanna know why every paparazzi wants to get something on me, but can't?" Cole asked as he looked at me with playful eyes.

"Why is that?" I asked.

"Because I don't do anything stupid like fall in love with another star and get married to them to only get a divorce in the end. Because that star would probably do something stupid, and I'd be in on the scandal. I rather just act for the enjoyment of acting for my fans and me. I don't do drugs or drink alcohol. I don't do anything that the normal stars do or did. I don't sleep around with sluts. It's fun to see people try to dig up dirt on me," Cole said with a big grin. "It's like a big treasure hunt for them, but, it's probably going to change soon enough."

"What do you mean?" *He was just talking about taking drugs and alcohol. Is he going to start doing those things? That wouldn't make sense.*

"You, Crystal Ann. I am bringing you to my house. Paparazzi are most likely going to be watching, and we're probably going to be in headlines tomorrow. They're going to think we're lovers."

I couldn't help but laugh out loud. "That's a funny way of putting it."

"But we both know it's true," he sighed as he leaned back. "I am kinda sorry I brought you here. I wish I could've kept you a secret a little bit longer."

"A secret?" I asked.

"So you wouldn't be hurt in that way I was almost hurt," he said.

"I am a reporter, Cole," I said, looking away from his gaze. "I am sure I can handle it." I sat up straighter as if I was trying to prove to Cole I could hold my own.

"I guess you'll have to see," Cole said solemnly.

The rest of the car ride was in silence. *I am a little scared of what can happen. Are these paparazzi really that crazy? I sure hope not.*

I gasped at the beauty of Cole's home when we drove up to it. The house had Grecian columns that held up the front porch. The big mansion was beautifully lit up. I noticed a fountain in his driveway with three bowls for the water that sat on top of each other, then the pool at the bottom. I was amazed at the many flowers and gardens around his home.

"How big is your house?" I asked.

"Eh. I'd have to look." Cole yawned. "I don't remember."

We pulled up close to the front door. A butler came down to my door, which was closer to the house. He opened the door and handed me a large coat.

"Master Dakota wished for you to be hidden if you so choose, in case there are people watching," the man offered kindly.

"Thank you, Kevin," Cole said as he opened up his own door and went to my side. "It's all right, Crystal Ann. I don't exactly want to reveal you yet."

"I almost sound like a prize," I sassed, though I felt uncertain.

"You are a beautiful prize to be won by none other than me, yes. I'd agree with you there." Cole spoke with a serious voice, but his eyes sparkled. I took the coat with haste and put it over my head.

"Lead me in," I said, glaring playfully at Cole as we walked into his home.

Inside his home was even more spectacular. It had beautiful granite floors with walls painted so it looked like it was plated in gold.

"Woah," I gasped as I looked up, seeing a massive chandelier that looked like diamonds. It sparkled as if the stars were shining during the day.

"Let me show you to your room," Cole said, smiling brightly.

"Okay." Kevin took the coat from me with a slight bow of his head as Cole led me down different hallways.

All of them were painted gold, until we reached a hallway where the walls were crimson red with gold vines running all around the walls.

"Woah," I gasped again at the beauty.

"I'm glad you like my house," Cole said with a small chuckle. I could feel him smiling in front of me. "You might say I have good taste, but really, my manager does. She told me I couldn't live in a small house because everyone like me has a big house, and what's a superstar without their mansion?" He shrugged. "I guess it's to keep up appearances but I really wouldn't mind living in a smaller house unless I have twenty kids running around."

"I think you should have what you want, but this house is beautiful and magnificent." The walls were bare, as the previous walls were, except for the designs. "It's so fun to look at." I smiled slightly, thinking of his comment about children. "I'm not sure you'd want twenty children though."

Cole chuckled. "I'm glad you think so, Crystal Ann."

He suddenly stopped, and I, not noticing, bumped right into his back. "Oh, sorry," I said as my nose throbbed in pain for a few moments. I held it to make sure it wouldn't start bleeding again.

"This will be your room." Cole opened the door. The room was pitch black until Cole turned on the light.

I blinked in astonishment as I looked at the room. The room was painted to look like space. "Oh my. . ." I softly gasped as I stepped in. The ceiling had the night sky painted on it. I saw a few star constellations as I looked for them. "This! Woah! This is spectacular!" I laughed, delighted as I looked toward the large queen-sized bed. The large comforter was designed to look like the surface of planet Earth, the throw pillows looked like the sun. I felt like crying because everything in this room seemed perfect.

"If you like this room, you should see my room," Cole teased.

"This room leaves me speechless," I whispered as I stood close to the door, not daring to walk inside without further permission.

"Would it be even cooler if I told you that the stars glow in the dark?"

"You're kidding," I said as I turned toward him. "Do they?"

"No," Cole said.

"Oh."

"We could make it that way, but, I didn't think you'd enjoy this room so much," Cole laughed lightheartedly.

"I love outer space. It's truly beautiful and amazing with what's out there in the galaxy," I stated. "When we get pictures of cosmic dust and other galaxies being formed— it's amazing!"

"Sounds like you should've been an astronomist," Cole said in a more serious tone, but he was still teasing.

"They're too smart for me, and I wasn't very good with math. Took me a while to get the concepts of anything math related," I shrugged, rolling my eyes. "But, this room is amazing. It's like I'm camping out and sleeping under the stars."

"I'm glad you like it, Crystal Ann," Cole said as he went to leave, but I stopped him.

"Are other rooms like this?" I asked.

"Only some. Not one room is the exact same. Other rooms are consistent with nature and other things. I mean, every room has a theme. Some of them are even based on certain movies."

"Phantom of the Opera?"

"One of my favorite movies, but sadly, that's what my living room is based on," he teased.

I wanted to squeal and go fangirl about how awesome his house was. It was truly amazing.

"Do you like *Phantom of the Opera?*" Cole asked.

"Only the movie adaption with Gerard Butler," I said. "I am not a really big fan other than that. I don't like how anyone else sounds when they sing the songs."

"That's all right. The movie adaption is really well done, for the time it was made," Cole said.

"You seem disappointed?"

"No. Not at all. Just tired, and hangry." he said.

"'Hangry'? What's 'hangry' mean?"

"Hungry—angry," Cole said. "Are you hungry?"

"A little bit, but excitement mostly filled me up. I'm so overwhelmed that I may not even be hungry."

Cole grinned. "All right. Let's go to the kitchen then?" he offered.

"Only if you make us food."

"Best I can do is a sandwich."

"All right," I giggled, following him.

Chapter Eleven

The water of the shower ran down my body as I stood underneath the head. The shower was so hot that steam fogged up the bathroom.

I finished rinsing the conditioner out of my hair and turned off the water. I grabbed a towel and wrapped it around me. I wiped some dew from the mirror, and saw a man with a camera and a sudden flash as he took a picture. I screamed as I turned around and saw the paparazzi.

"Who are you? What do you want? Why were you watching me?" I shouted, terrified.

"I finally got a picture exposing the famous Crystal Ann!" the man laughed and reached for my towel.

"Cole!" my voice echoed through the bathroom.

I gasped as my eyes popped open. I shot up, sweating slightly. I blinked quickly. The dream seemed all too real. I lifted a hand to my forehead as I moaned. *What was that about?* I sighed as I laid back down into the memory foam pillows that were warm from my body heat. I put the blanket over my head, making the Earth blanket look more round than it was before. *Ugh. What was that dream?*

Is it because of what Cole said yesterday? About the paparazzi breaking into his house? I don't know.

I pushed the blanket away and saw that it was a few minutes to six.

I got out of bed, grabbed my toothbrush along with my comb and made my way into the bathroom connected to my room.

The bathroom wasn't a continuation of space décor; it was a deep underwater theme like Atlantis, or what I imagined to be Atlantis.

I brushed my teeth and hair, deciding not to take a shower in case my dream came true. *That'd be terrifying. Being exposed like that in public may be one of my worst fears and anxieties.*

I let out a comforting sigh as the fear passed. I walked out of my room as a maid walked past.

"Good morning, Miss Alston," she said with a Latina accent. I got a better look at her after a few blinks, forcing the blurry vision out of my eyes. She was smiling from ear to ear.

"G-Good morning," I responded kindly. She smiled at me as she continued to dust the walls.

"Oh, hello, Crystal Ann," Cole said on the other side of me.

I looked up and saw his smiling face. "Good morning."

Cole smiled down at me. "Did you sleep well?"

"Yes," I said. "That bathroom is especially nice."

Cole nodded. "I'd agree. It's one of my favorite rooms for my favorite people. I hardly have anyone stay in there."

"I am glad I have a special privilege then," I grinned as we both laughed.

We walked down the hallway in silence, but our smiles seemed to be echoing within the hallways. *I don't know how to explain this feeling of warmth inside my heart that's spreading through my veins. I wonder how far deep his feelings go. I know they're far down enough to bring me here to get to know me better, but, how far do they really go? Is this a crush? Is he acting on a whim? I'm so uncertain.*

When we got to the dining room, breakfast was there for the both of us.

"I'm surprised you didn't get up earlier," I said, truthfully.

"Jet lag," Cole chuckled as we sat down.

"I think I'm feeling it," I yawned as I picked up my fork, and then realized that I had already brushed my teeth. I paused for a moment. *Is this going to taste gross? I should drink some water first to help get rid of the awful taste I know I'm going to taste on my tongue.*

"You all right?" Cole had already dug in.

"I realized that I had brushed my teeth. It was out of habit."

"Just eat!" he said in a playful voice. "This'll be the only day I can take you to Disneyland."

"You really don't have—" I started, but got cut off.

"But I want to!" He smiled kindly as he continued to eat.

I slowly began to eat, and the dreadful taste touched my tongue as I ate the sweet eggs. My muscles tensed in my face. I hurriedly swallowed my eggs. I grabbed the orange juice but feared that drinking this orange juice would make it worse.

"Is there any place where I could grab some water?" I started to stand but was stopped by a kind butler who sat me back down.

"I will get it for you, Miss Alston." He left for only a moment and came back with a cold water bottle. "For the miss," he said as he placed it beside my plate on the table.

"Thank you." I drank some water quickly, pushing back the minty taste.

"You sure you're fine?" Cole said softly, noticing I was struggling a bit.

"Yeah, just that gross flavor of mint and sweet eggs." I continued to eat. The taste of the mint-sweet flavor subsided as the sweet eggs took over my mouth. *Sweet eggs for the past week have been good, but I think they may get tiring soon.*

"If you have us eat sweet eggs too often we'll get tired of them," I said as I finished up my eggs.

Cole gave a slow nod as he thought about it. "I guess you're right. I'll think of something else for tomorrow morning's breakfast."

"If you say so," I said as I stood.

"I do say so. Jaquk!" Cole said.

A butler came into the room; he was a young and tall man. His eyes gleamed as he gave us a subtle smile.

"Please, bring the car around."

"Yes, sir." He left quickly.

We slowly walked out to the front, and when Cole opened the door for us, there sat a little car. I gazed up at him. It wasn't an expensive car. It was an old beat-up one with scratched paint. It was most definitely a lemon. "Is this your car?" I asked, confused.

Cole gave me a serious look. "Yes, it is," he said. "If we're going to go to Disneyland incognito, then we need a car that doesn't seem expensive."

"Oh," I giggled. "Did you beat it up yourself?"

"It's amazing what an angry woman can do," he said as his regular smile came back to his lips.

"An ex-girlfriend?"

"No, but if it was, it'd probably be Taylor Swift," he said in a very serious voice, but we both burst out laughing.

"Have you ever tried dating her?" I rubbed my eyes to make sure I didn't start crying from laughing too hard.

"No," Cole said. "I wouldn't want to go down in history as one of her breakup songs. I don't really know her either. She seems nice, but I have heard she's a bit crazy."

I nodded. "I don't listen to her music often, but I've liked how she's done things so far."

Cole didn't say anything as he opened my door for me. I quickly climbed in. He closed the door, went around to the other side, got in, and turned the car over. "You excited?" he asked.

"I'd be excited if you let me interview you," I teased, hinting at the real reason I was here in the first place.

"I only dragged you out here because I thought you were cute," he said in a high-pitched voice.

I laughed as he kept going.

"I only want to see Crystal Ann smile and laugh," he said as he pinched his nose, making his voice go even higher. "I want to get to know her better, and see if she is the clumsy girl I met outside of the Starbucks." He coughed after he cleared his throat.

"I'm guessing it's hard to do that voice?"

"Just a little bit, but it makes you laugh, so it's worth it," he winked as he kept his eyes on the road.

"There are so many people here."

"There are a lot of people in New York too," Cole commented.

"That's true." I shrugged. "But these people just seem different, somehow."

"Really?"

"Yeah," I said as I focused on some of the large palm trees that we were rushing past. "How long until Disney?"

"It's about fifty-five minutes from my place," he said.

My jaw fell open. "Fifty-five minutes?"

"Are you excited, little one?" he chuckled, teasing me.

"Well, maybe just a little bit," I said truthfully. "I haven't been to Disneyland. It's only been a dream until now."

"Well, Disneyland is the land where dreams come true," Cole said in a serious voice.

I folded my arms over my chest. "Wow," I said.

"What?" Cole asked.

"I—I can't believe you used their theme against me," I teased, as if I were upset.

We both chuckled as I leaned back into my seat. The both of us sat in silence, but it wasn't awkward. It was a warm silence. For some reason, this silence was comforting.

"The news said that it's going to be a cool day today," Cole said. "With gentle winds coming from the west."

"We both know that a weatherman isn't always right."

He snorted as he tried not to grin. "Well, if it's hot, you'll have to leave," Cole said.

"Why is that?" I asked, not understanding the joke.

"To make it cool," he said, his grin disappearing.

"What do you mean by that?" I asked, confused. *I don't know where this could be going. Unless it's a misleading compliment like the cute dude on Vine that makes it sound like he's going to rip a person open but then gives them a compliment and laughs about it. Thomas Sanders, I think.*

"Because you're *too hot* to be around," Cole said as he looked at me dead in the eye for a split moment, before turning back to the road.

Before I could respond with anything else, he braked.

"Oof," I said as my body pushed against the seatbelt, then back into my seat. "What was that?" I asked, rubbing my chest where the seatbelt had dug into me.

"Had to stop for a kid," Cole said. "Didn't see him until the last second."

"Thank you!" said the kid from outside the car, with a little wave, as he finished crossing the street.

Cole waved at the boy, and at the last moment, after we had already started going, the boy realized who Cole was. The boy waved happily again, and his face seemed like it would smile for the rest of his life.

"I'm guessing he ran across the street."

"Yeah, I hate it when kids do that. They're so hard to see," Cole sighed.

"They're so tiny, it's understandable," I said with a small smile.

*

I screamed at the top of my lungs as we began to descend from the top of the tower. I grabbed onto my safety harness as tightly as I could. We stopped falling and were taken back up, then dropped again. My heart was racing the whole time as I continued to fall and rise back up until we reached the ground. *If this were a cartoon, my hair would be straight like cardboard and all over the place.*

Cole stretched as we got off the Tower of Terror in Disneyland. My heart was still racing, and my face was green, or at least feeling green.

"You all right?" he asked, as if it were nothing.

"I think I lost half of my soul," I could barely breathe. My knees trembled every so often as I stood.

"You two are going to have to hustle out for the next group," the Disney cast member said in a kind, but hurried tone.

"C'mon, Crystal Ann," Cole said as he took my arm and led me out. "I'm guessing you didn't enjoy it?"

"Unsure." I breathed deeply. "I mean, maybe after the adrenaline rush is gone, I might like it and want to go on it again. B-But not right now."

Cole rubbed my back. "We can go on the Dumbo ride, if you want," Cole suggested.

"That looks a little scary too." I stood up straight, still trying to catch my breath.

Cole chuckled as he put his arm around my shoulders and gave me a caring look. "I would ride with you, but it's a one-person ride, so you're going to have to be strong and ride this ride either in front of me or beside me. I promise I won't let you fall alone."

I think it's nice that he's so kind to me. It's a nice break for my heart. Everyone in the city is just so mean, only rooting for themselves; they stomp on people to get to the top, and it's all for money. This world makes me sad, but when I look at Cole . . . That . . . Well . . . He brightens up my world, and I don't know if I could be without him and his kind heart.

"So, did you really post the picture of us from the Statue of Liberty on your social media?" I asked, out of the blue, after I had caught my breath.

"I thought you'd be following me by now," Cole chuckled, but then he saw I was serious. His goofy smile turned into one that was caring as he looked down at me. "No, I haven't," he said, shaking his head. "I don't know if I should introduce you to my fans. I mean, some of them are crazy and would attack you."

I gave a nervous chuckle as I looked away. "Yeah, I guess some girls are like that."

"Some men are like that too, ya' know," Cole said, in a more serious voice.

"Oh, sorry," I said apologetically. "You're right. How crazy are men at protecting you?"

Cole gave a nervous chuckle and a look of horror. "Very protective if they don't 'ship' it."

"Ship it?"

"It's hard to explain if you don't know," Cole said, thinking.

I sat in silence as I waited for him to answer my question.

"When you see two people in a show, or maybe even in real life, you can 'ship it' just because you think they'd be cute and compatible together."

"Oh," I said, not shocked. "So, what you're saying is that you're not gay?"

"No, I am not," Cole said, calmly. "But, just because I'm not gay doesn't mean I don't love gay people as much as straight people."

"I see."

"Are you lesbian?" Cole asked in a serious tone.

"No, I don't see anything wrong with them, though."

"But, would you still love someone if they were? Like your sister."

"Yes, of course I would!" I stated in a sober voice as I looked up at Cole. "I get your point."

"Yeah, you probably do . . . "

"Something else on your mind?" I asked.

"I just feel like I should say something to you, Crystal Ann," he said, looking at me for a moment.

"Go ahead."

"Even if we ever disagree on something . . . Maybe religion or sexual orientation or even something trivial. For example, how we like our toilet paper facing. It won't stop me from fighting for what you believe in, even if I don't practice it." Cole said. A small smile came to his face as he continued to walk me around the park.

I couldn't help but smirk as I wrote down a few of his words in the notebook I carried around in my bag.

"I can't believe you're working and writing down our private conversation," Cole teased.

"You should know that what you say aloud is never private," I snickered as I finished up my notes on our conversation.

Cole raised his eyebrows in a playful manner. "Stop proving me wrong."

I couldn't help but laugh as I shook my head. We continued around the park and played at Disneyland.

Chapter Twelve

The sun began to set as we rode the *Pirates of the Caribbean* ride. When we came out, the red-and-orange-lined sunset had faded into a dark purple, the color of night.

I folded my arms and looked toward the west, where the sun had just set.

"What is it, Crystal Ann?" Cole asked.

I looked over and up at him with a small smile. "I wanted to take a picture of the sunset, but I didn't get a chance to, because there were too many people to take a good photo."

"Tomorrow will have another sunset." Cole put his hands onto my shoulders in comfort.

I raised my eyebrow in a playful manner. "You should stop trying to make me feel better."

Cole chuckled as he took his hands away from my shoulders and walked in front of me. "Okay, okay. Why don't we go see the fireworks show, then?" He asked. "Will that make up for missing the sunset?"

I pretended to think for a moment as I hummed, looking around at the darkening sky. No stars were visible, due to the lights. I pretended to think. "Fine," I said, as if it were out of the way.

Cole took my hand. "If I may." He began to lead me toward Cinderella's castle.

As we began to walk, we heard what sounded like a gunshot, then a little screech. Suddenly, an explosion of color lit up the night as if it was day. I couldn't deny that my heart was racing as many more fireworks went up.

"Oh, wow," I gasped as many different colors touched my eyes. My small grin grew into a big, goofy smile as I clapped my hands, as if I were a satisfied small child. I jumped up and down. "This is amazing!" I shouted as I looked up at Cole. He was already looking at me, smiling and chuckling.

"You really do enjoy fireworks, then?" he asked.

"Yes, I do," I said. "I love fireworks!" I felt my heart pumping fast. My hands began to sweat as I had started to lose my momentum from jumping up and down constantly. I fell into Cole's arms.

"You need to be careful, Crystal Ann," he laughed as he held me in his arms, looking down at me, helping me back onto my feet.

"Sorry," I apologized. My flushed cheeks went unnoticed in the reds, greens, blues, and purples exploding in the darkness.

"Just don't want you to get hurt," he said softly. He let me go as I turned toward the fireworks. "It'll last about. . . fourteen to fifteen minutes. Let's hang tight."

We stood in silence for the rest of the firework show. "It's time to start heading home," Cole whispered as the fireworks stopped shooting up into the sky.

"Okay."

"Are you tired?" he asked.

I yawned as he asked, then I looked up at him. "A lil' bit," I said, yawning again. "I just need to stretch."

"Do you want me to carry you?" he asked.

I giggled. "I'm not a little girl."

"Well, you're shorter than I am. You are also female. I say you are a smaller girl than I am." He suddenly swept me off my feet, and I was in his arms.

"Put me down!" I demanded as my heart beat harshly against my chest from embarrassment.

"What if I say no?" he asked.

"That's being selfish and maybe even mean," I stated, trying to get him to put me down. He continued to laugh as he put me down onto my feet. I walked forward, catching my breath and trying to get my racing heart to calm down.

"Didn't know that would count as selfish," he called after me.

"The only reason you should carry me is if I'm hurt," I said in a light but serious tone. "I am a grown 'girl' after all, even if I am 'smaller' than you." I nodded my head, as if satisfied with my refute to his statement.

"And you know that it's really no big deal," he laughed as I let him catch up to me. He put his arm around my shoulders.

"Is this necessary?" I asked.

He looked at me with a raised eyebrow, his eyes telling me that he was trying to be playful.

"We need to be cautious of those around us," he said. "We may be in a park for families but we still need to stick together in the park. You could get lost, and I wouldn't want that to happen. You still have your job to do."

I put my arm around his waist, pulling myself closer to him. "Only this one time," I whispered.

"Yes!" He held me close, and we walked to the car. He opened my door for me again and closed it when I had gotten in. I put my seatbelt on as I yawned again. I began to gaze out the window once more.

"You can sleep on the way back. It's an hour-long drive," Cole said as he pulled out of the parking lot and onto the street.

"Wouldn't want you to feel alone," I whispered as I was falling asleep.

"If you are going to sleep, at least put your seat down," he said as I closed my heavy eyes.

I pulled the lever and gently put the seat down into a lying position. My eyes felt heavy for the last time as I went to sleep.

"Crystal Ann," I heard Cole say from my dreams. I moaned in response to being awoken. I barely opened my eyes for a moment and saw Cole's face in front of mine. I felt like I was moving but I couldn't tell. He felt so warm.

"Cole," I tried to whisper, but my lips wouldn't move, and Cole didn't respond. This was a pleasant dream, so I cuddled more into Cole's arm. My fingers gently grasped his shirt sleeve as I continued to sleep.

I felt as if the sun was hugging me. I could feel myself smile as the dream continued to be so lovely. The clouds held me and gently soared with me in their arms.

Chapter Thirteen

Steam followed me out of the bathroom as I continued to towel dry my hair. I got dressed, and a knock came to my door as I put my dirty clothes away into my suitcase.

"Crystal Ann?" Cole's voice spoke from the other side.

"It's unlocked," I informed him as I closed my suitcase and watched him walk in from the corner of my eye.

"It's going to be another busy day today," he said. He paused for a moment, looking around the room. "It's hot and humid in here," he spoke playfully as he began to fan himself.

"I took a very, very hot bath to relax my muscles from yesterday," I said, speaking of Disneyland. *It was fun, but I was on my feet all day, and I am still sore.*

"Oh, does that help?" he asked.

"For me," I shrugged, unsure about whether it would help him or not. "When are we leaving?"

"We'll have to skip breakfast to get there on time. I'm sure they'll have a food table," Cole said with a small smile.

"That's fine," I nodded professionally.

Cole gave me a bit of a disappointed look as I watched him step out of the room. His phone rang.

"One moment," he said to me as he answered. He immediately began to argue; he told the person on the phone that he was sorry and that he had slept in. I knew he was lying. He was waiting for me.

"Cole," I said, trying to get his attention but he gave me his index finger, signaling me to give him a moment. I backed off. I brought my hair out to the side and braided it carefully. I stared at Cole pacing in the hallway, as his words seem to blur together while my mind began to wonder. I was lost in looking at him.

"Let's go, Crystal Ann." Cole said playfully. He held out his hand to me.

I smiled as I took his hand and leaned into his lips. I could feel my pinkie twitch, but I didn't care.

"Crystal Ann," Cole said. I came out of my fog and looked up at Cole with a serious expression.

"We going now?"

"Yes, we're late. We need to hurry," he said, turning away. I knew he was mad because his eyes had flames in them. The fire was spreading everywhere, uncontained.

"Cole?"

"Yeah?"

"Do you want to hear a joke?" I asked as I followed behind him.

I could feel his frustration ease at my words, but I'd noticed the flame in his eyes was still burning. I carefully walked up beside him. *I have no idea how to calm him down, but I'll just have to act cute or something.*

"Go ahead and tell me, Crystal Ann," he gently said.

"A home improvements man is hired to take down a makeshift wall in the attic in Titusville, Florida. Upon breaking a hole to find out what was hidden behind the wall, a human skeleton was discovered. Police were called in to investigate. DNA was taken from the remains for analysis." I began.

"Okay," he said, raising his eyebrow, not knowing what to expect. He led me to a really nice car.

"Wow, this is a nice car," I said.

"It is," Cole said with a small smile. My eyes grew wide with admiration for the Corvette that sat in front of me.

"I don't know if I feel worthy enough to sit in it," I stated seriously as my smile faded. I looked at the passenger seat through the window in wonder.

Cole chuckled as he walked over to me. He patted my shoulder, opening my door for me. "You first, m'lady."

"Oh, no, I can't." I backed into his chest.

"I don't want to have to kidnap you. C'mon," he whispered in my ear. "You still need my interview."

My heart beat quickly against my chest. "Are you sure? I feel as if I'd ruin it." I was uncertain, taking a quick glimpse at Cole then back at the seat.

"Cars are meant to be run and driven. It's all right," he said. "Just sit down. I'm sure you won't ruin it more than I have."

"Okay." I got into the car; he closed the door after I got in. I buckled as Cole got in the driver side.

"You want to continue your joke, now?" he asked turning over the car.

"What joke?" I asked as I looked up, having completely forgotten about the joke I was telling him. I was holding the seat belt tightly. *I have never, ever, ever been this close to a nice car like this.*

"About the skeleton behind the wall. The police were investigating the DNA," he explained.

"Oh!" I said, remembering. "I'm sure it's ruined now."

"No, just tell me the ending. I have a quirk for needing to hear or see the ending of anything." he explained.

"All right. Do you want me to start over?" I asked.

"No," he said, shaking his head. "I remember. Just tell me."

"Okay," I said, thinking where I left off. "The results of the DNA test determined that the corpse was that of the 1987 National Champion of 'Hide and Go Seek'," I said.

Cole snickered as he rolled his eyes. I clenched the seat belt tightly as he drove the car smoothly out of his garage. "That was a bad joke," he laughed.

"It at least made you smile."

"Thank you."

"For what?" I looked up at him instead of at my lap.

"Thank you," he repeated to himself.

I smiled back. "You're very welcome, then," I responded as I loosened up.

*

My eyes widened as I gasped and smiled. "Wow," I exclaimed as I got out of the car. "It's so huge!"

"Have you never been to a studio set before?" he asked.

"No, I really haven't." He led me inside the huge studio where there was a ton of people. "Woah." I gasped. "There's a lot of lights here." I looked around, fascinated by everyone and everything.

Cole couldn't help but laugh at my ignorance. "It's pretty big."

"Cole!" Rachel said, coming up to us.

"Hello, Rachel. Good morning," he said, almost as if in a sarcastic tone. He folded his arms in reservation across his chest.

"You're late! You know that you can get fired from this job." she murmured so only Cole and I could hear.

I raised my eyebrows. "Hello, I'm Crystal Ann."

"I'm aware," she said. "I am Rachel. We've met."

"Oh," I said breathlessly. Her brazen way of speaking kept my personality from coming forward. I put my arms uncomfortably at my sides.

Cole glanced back at me then back at Rachel. "You're making her uncomfortable. You should at least try to be a *little* nice."

"Sorry," she apologized to me, glaring at Cole. "I just want to make sure your 'job'," she said, using her fingers, "doesn't get in the way of Cole's job. I can't let that happen."

"I see," I whispered. "I understand." I clenched my teeth. *I don't know why, but I feel so offended by how she is talking down to me. Well, I guess it's okay to feel a little defensive if I'm feeling this way, right?*

"I wish Cole wouldn't have played with you and brought you here. He doesn't have time," Rachel sighed.

My eyebrows rose as my heart gave a sudden jump. It began to sink like the Titanic." I am only doing my job," I stated in a strong voice, standing straighter, crossing my arms, and standing with my hip popped out.

"It's your job to run around?" Rachel asked with a small laugh.

I smiled. "It's my job to run around and get a story if my boss wishes it, and I am only following orders."

"Like a little lamb?"

"Yes. That is my job, isn't it? Just like your job is to manage Cole's famous life, but it is his decision if he wants to be a part of a production."

"Which, I would love to be a part of this one," Cole said, trying to appease Rachel with his words before trying to appease me. "I've read through the script a few times, and it seems like it'll be a nice movie." He was trying to make peace, but I was completely calm and able to hold back my fury.

"Well, I'll help see to it that Cole does sit down with you for an interview after today, as to not inconvenience you by keeping you here for a long time," Rachel said, looking me up and down. Her eyes narrowed slightly.

"Don't worry," I said. "My plane ticket is all ready for me to return to New York, but if Mr. Dakota is too busy to let me interview him now, then I understand. I will continue to wait patiently because that's both what I need to do and what was asked of me."

"So, I'm going to go to the dressing room," Cole said, pulling me along. "I want her to interview other people so she has stuff to do."

"Whatever," Rachel said. I saw her nostrils flare ever so slightly as she turned around and walked away without another word.

"She's . . . very bold," Cole said as he walked to two women. He sat down in the seat in the middle of them.

"I picked up on that." I took out my notepad as make-up artists began to put makeup on him.

"Who is this, Cole?" asked one of them as they looked at me.

"I'm Miss Alston. A reporter from the New York Times," I said, professionally. "Mr. Dakota has asked me to conduct an exclusive interview with him, and he has yet to answer any of my questions because he wants the perfect location to do this, but I don't even have a camera man. I'll just be getting his voice."

"That's so like you, Cole," one laughed, dabbing foundation onto his face. They both immediately began to blend foundation a shade lighter into his tanned skin.

"May I ask you two a few questions as you are doing his makeup or should I wait?" I asked, finding and taking a seat in front of Cole and behind the makeup artists.

"Sure! Ask away!" said one.

I hummed as I thought of what I could ask. *Now that I have the opportunity to ask any question I like, I can't think of anything to ask! Why does this always happen? My mind . . . I swear my brain farts too often. Maybe I should just ask simple questions. This is all about Cole anyway . . . I just need to ask about Cole. That's it! That's good. I'm good.*

"Do you enjoy working with Mr. Dakota?" I asked, trying to keep my professionalism.

"Yes," one said. I wrote down phrases I thought would fit in my article. "He's fun to be around and he cheers up everyone's day . . . But there are those days where he's just a monster."

"Don't tell her that. She might run away scared," Cole said, a little disappointed at the woman's honesty.

"Well, I need you to look more human than you are, Mr. Angel," the makeup artist laughed, knowing he was a bit upset with her.

"What's your name? I never caught it," I said, looking up at her and wishing I could ignore their conversation.

"My name is Lucy. My sister's name is Ava," she said, gesturing toward the other make-up artist.

"Oh! So you two are sisters!" I said with a small smile.

"Do you have siblings?" asked Ava.

"Yes, I do," I said. "My sister." I tried to keep my emotions calm as I brought my sister up, hoping the thoughts of her would go away.

"Siblings just suck sometimes, don't they?" Lucy laughed.

I softly snorted as I continued to write down what they were saying in my notes. I tried to keep everything about Cole in my notes, but they were so funny and went off topic often. It was hard to stay on the right path. In the middle of our conversation, Cole left to go film as I talked with them. He seemed quiet and maybe even flustered with how I was asking questions about him. *I'm not sure that he really was upset.*

"You should go watch how he acts," Lucy said.

"Yeah," Ava said. "You should take notes at how he acts and how many times he has to do a scene. He's a really good actor."

"All right," I said. "It was nice talking to you two."

"Yeah!" Lucy said with a big smile.

"Anytime." Ava spoke, turning around and gathering up the makeup.

As they did their job, I carefully and silently did mine. I walked over toward the director behind the camera. I was silent as a ninja and as observant as a librarian. *I wonder why I even think sometimes . . .*

"Woah!" The director said suddenly as he looked over toward me. "CUT! Who are you?"

"I'm Miss Alston," I said. "I'm here interviewing Mr. Dakota, and he brought me here."

"Well, you don't have to stay here. You're probably going to be a distraction. Personally, I don't want you here due to privacy reasons," the director said.

"Hey, Joe, it's all right." Cole said, coming behind him.

"No, it's not, Cole. You shouldn't have brought her here and you know it." Joe, the director, warned.

"I'm only doing a story on Mr. Dakota. If I wished to know what your movie was about I would go to Wikipedia to find the information. Information gets leaked either way. But I am not here to leak your new movie. I am to interview Mr. Dakota, but he keeps putting me off," I responded calmly and collectedly. "If you really need more convincing, I can sign a nondisclosure that holds me to secrecy until the movie comes out."

The two of them sat in silence, Cole looking at Joe with uncertainty and Joe looking at him with the same expression. "We've got to keep rolling, sir," Joe's assistant said.

"I will leave if you wish it, sir, but Mr. Dakota is my ride," I stated with a little grin.

Joe huffed. "Just be quiet and observe, then," he said, turning back toward the scene. "Get into place, Cole. I'll scold you later!" He turned to me for a moment. "I'll have you sign those papers on the way out."

Cole chuckled underneath his breath as he went back to his place.

I stayed completely quiet during the next scene. It was a scene similar to how Cole and I met, but it was a deli shop. He was the man behind the bar, helping the other actress ordering a sandwich. It went smoothly; nothing really happened except talking.

After the female began laughing, the director yelled, "Cut!" He got up and began to talk to the actors as he approached them, telling them how he wanted them to act and such. I wasn't sure what he was saying; he was talking much too fast.

A woman came up to me with a director's chair and placed it next to Joe's chair. She motioned for me to come over to the chair.

"I didn't think that you'd like to stand the whole time," she shyly said as she let me sit down.

"Thank you," I smiled with a small nod. She seemed nice.

Joe came back. "Actors sometimes." He shook his head, rolling his eyes to himself, climbing back into his chair.

"Ah, yes," I said with a small nod. *People can't help but want to speak to me. Maybe this is one of the reasons I'm a reporter.* "Actors can be a pain, but it's worth it in the end, isn't it?" I asked.

"Maybe. Let's hope I pull enough strings to make teenage girls go crazy over it. So much that they'll all come to see it."

"It's that bad, huh?"

The director lifted his eyebrows but shook his head and told everyone to get into place. He didn't seem to like what I had said. *He wouldn't have to use sex appeal if it was a good movie. These are the kinds of movies I don't go see because they have eye candy and no real story.*

"From the top!" The director leaned back in his chair and crossed his legs.

I looked from the director to Cole. It seemed that he was trying his hardest to please this man. It also seemed he wasn't enjoying himself as much as he would've liked. "Hmm," I hummed softly. I could feel the director's eyes pierce my soul as he looked to me.

"Cut!" the director called. "What is it?" he asked me, intrigued.

"Mr. Dakota doesn't seem to be enjoying himself," I spoke truthfully.

Everyone's eyes focused on the director and me as he folded his arms, coming out of his chair.

"He looks perfectly fine to me!" he argued.

"Let me talk to Mr. Dakota," I said, ignoring the director, I walked toward Cole. He began walking toward me as well.

"What are you doing?" Cole asked, in a whisper.

"You're not enjoying yourself," I said. "That makes your acting bad."

"This is a job. I don't need to enjoy it."

"I know," I said. "But, I can tell that you're supposed to fall in love with your opposite in this scene. That is what the director is looking for and he's not getting it. Your eyes aren't telling the truth. I know that if you think of her face as the face of someone you love deeply, then you're going to get the shot the director wants."

"Do you really think so?" A small smile came to his face.

"I know so." I nodded as I turned away, going back to my seat.

"What did you say to him?" the director asked, his eyebrow still raised at me.

"Words of encouragement," I said with a little smile. I folded my leg over the other and watched.

The director hesitated, then told everyone to get into place.

As the scene began, I couldn't help but smile, knowing that this was what the director was looking for.

*

"Man, this is hard stuff," I sighed as I stuffed some food into my mouth.

"Acting isn't all fun and games," Cole scanned the table but didn't pick anything up. There seemed to be nothing he wanted to eat.

"I could figure that," I said, between bites of food. "Reporting isn't all fun and games either." I finally swallowed my food. "You have to chase your story no matter what to ensure you get it. I mean, I've been chasing you around for nearly two weeks so you can give me what you wanted to be made public."

"Reporting seems hard too," he said, with a tiny smile on the sides of his lips.

"Harder than you'd think it is, yes," I said, nodding. "You not hungry?" I asked.

"I don't usually eat with the staff or pick off this table. I enjoy my own cooking more."

"Interesting," I said, quickly taking out my notepad.

"Do you really have to get that out?" he sighed, upset that I was working.

"Well, you're not giving me a story to write about so I'm just going to write about you, personally." I gave him a warning.

"Please, Crystal Ann, just stop," he begged.

I looked up at him, confused. My smile turned fake and nearly unbearable to keep up. I put my notepad away into my pocket. I looked up at him as nicely as I could.

"I can't just vacation for two weeks and not get the story that I was promised, Mr. Dakota," I said.

"It's Cole."

"I know, but you suddenly want to seem professional. Or do you want to get personal?" I asked a bit curtly. "What's wrong?" I spoke in a soft voice.

"It's nothing," he said. I knew he was not trying to worry me, but the situation was killing the joy of working with him.

"You're obviously having a hard time keeping it to yourself, and you're letting me see it."

"I'm really trying not to," Cole chuckled, trying to brush it off. "You can just see right through me. You're just too good."

"Interesting," I responded. "Well, I hope to sit down with you tonight in your living room so you can give me your promised interview."

Cole looked away at the set. "I guess so, Crystal Ann," he said.

I said nothing more. *I wish he'd depend on me a little bit. I am not going to publish every single detail that's happened between us. I wouldn't do that to his private life, but he came to me and my boss wants me to do this, and I intend to do a pleasant job for him and for my boss. But he's not letting me interview him to get my job done.*

I wish I knew how to interact with him better. It'd make this a lot easier.

Chapter Fourteen

"Please, Mr. Dakota," I said, pressing the record button on my recording device and set it down in between us. "Is Cole Dakota your real name?" I asked.

"Yes, it is, actually. I'm glad my agent liked it," he laughed. I couldn't help but smile. *I know he is forcing himself, but I leave tomorrow evening, and I really need this done.*

"Yes, that is always a good thing, Mr. Dakota. Can you tell me a little bit more about yourself?" I questioned.

"What would you like to know, Miss Alston?" he asked me. For the first time since learning my name, he didn't say my first name.

My eyebrows rose slightly at his snarky remark. I couldn't help but feel a little awkward with him talking professionally to me. He had never done that with me.

"Tell me about your childhood. How did you become a star? How was your family life?" I asked.

Cole began to speak as if he had rehearsed what he was going to say. He spoke about good memories and how he wasn't one of those people that grew up in too bad of a home. He seemed almost perfect.

As he was speaking, I thought back to my own childhood. My home was always filled with anger and contention. Everyone was always yelling at each other—constantly in arguments and fighting over whose doll was whose. *He makes his family almost sound perfect.*

"Was there anything wrong with your family, Mr. Dakota?" I asked, suddenly.

He seemed to be taken by surprise by my question. "What do you mean?" he asked.

"Did you never get into a fight with your dad or have bad friends?"

"Uh," he said, looking away, thinking. He was silent for many moments before he spoke. "I've had bad friends before. I mean, everyone has them. That is something you can't run away from—bad friends, I mean." Cole said, softly. He was thinking deeply. "I mean, some of them went to jail for being drug dealers, but I didn't associate with them when they became such a thing." Cole shrugged, not knowing what to say.

"All right," I said, leaning back in my chair. "Tell me about your school life."

Cole gave a nod and began to speak to me about how his school life was. I scribbled down what he said in my notes. Mine was miserable. My friends were constantly saying that they didn't want to be friends with me. Then before long, they would want to become friends with me again because they knew I would forgive them.

My sister ignored me when I tried to play with her and her friends. Well, that was in elementary school. I stayed by myself throughout middle school, being the number-one loner in school. I didn't bother to socialize. Partially because no one wanted to talk to me and, in all reality, I didn't want to talk to them either.

When other people started to form relationships, I was alone because I was never in any kind of group. I never took drama, choir, band, or any other fun classes, at least until high school. I just wanted to earn my credits and leave. I never had fun at school until my senior year. Even then, I never had a best friend, or at least someone I could call a best friend. I had a lot of acquaintances because those people already had a group of friends, and I had lost my chance to join them.

"That sounds like it was a little hard," I said to Cole's response to my question.

"Yeah," Cole said. "It was hard transferring to a school where I knew no one, and they constantly said that my acting was nothing," he chuckled. "Look at me now, though." He stopped laughing as he stared off.

"Is there something else that happened, Mr. Dakota?" I asked.

"Just remembering, is all," he said softly. "Can we take a little break?"

"If that's what you need," I said, stopping the recording. "Did I touch a sore spot, Cole?" I asked softly, looking toward him with concern.

"No," he said, giving a little fake laugh.

"You can tell me the truth."

"The truth might scare you away." He stood and went to his kitchen.

I stayed in my seat, looking toward the doorway. "It's all right if you don't want to tell me, but you need to tell me something," I informed him, the words just slipping out of my mouth. I stood up, walking toward the kitchen.

He set down his glass of water. He looked back up at me, as if he were thinking deeply about what to say and how to say it.

"I hate interviews," Cole admitted with a shake of his head. He walked up to me, putting a hand on my shoulder.

"I guessed that," I chuckled, taking a step forward, toward him. "You put me off for two weeks. I leave tomorrow."

"You did enjoy yourself, didn't you?" he asked, softly. His happy demeanor seemed to be dead today.

"I did enjoy my two weeks of fun," I stated, trying to get him to smile as I gave him a little giggle.

Cole returned a plaintive smile. He slowly brought me into a hug. I silently hugged him back. I felt it. I felt his love for me, and my love for him.

Tears came to my eyes as I felt a few of his tears fall down my neck. Mine did the same as I closed my eyes to take in his warmth.

"Do you want to go out and get some hot chocolate or something?"

"No, not really," he said, pulling away and turning his back to me.

"Then, is there anything you want to do?" I gently touched his shoulder.

"Not really. Movies sound like a good escape right now, though."

"All right. Let's watch any movie that you want to watch." I smiled.

I walked over to the table in the living room, grabbing my tape recorder before Cole led me to his theater room.

"What do you want to watch?" he asked.

"What movies do you have?"

He chuckled and took my hand. He led me to a closet. He turned on the light, and as the room lit up, I saw a movie collection that seemed like a million movies. *A walk-in closet of movies. Brilliant idea, Cole!*

"Wow!" I said, as I walked into the movie closet.

"I will ask that we don't watch any movies with me in them," he said with a shy smile. "It's kinda weird watching myself on screen."

"I understand." I looked around and found a few movies. I brought them out into his theater room and sat them down on a table.

I put five movies down. One was *Robin Hood*, the cartoon classic from Disney, in case he wanted a light mood. The second was *A Monster Calls*, in case he wanted to let his tears out. The next one I placed down was *Everest*, in case he wanted to watch a thriller. Another one I placed down was *The Phantom of the Opera* with Gerard Butler, in case he wanted to watch my favorite musical of all time. The last one I put down was *The Forest*, in case if he wanted to scare his own pants off.

"A lot of good choices," Cole said.

"I agree. You pick."

"Let's watch Robin Hood," he said, grabbing the DVD case and going to his projector at the top of the room. He set everything up as I sat myself on a large lounging chair and closed my eyes, dozing off.

Chapter Fifteen

I looked up at Cole. We stayed silent on the car ride to the airport. He gave me a small look before looking away. I gazed out the window. The magnificent dream I was having was coming to an end.

After so many minutes of the music playing in the car, I turned it off and looked at Cole. "I just want to thank you very much for giving me this opportunity to let—" I began.

"Please, don't go acting like this is something professional or a goodbye, Crystal Ann," he whispered. *He seems really torn about me leaving. Although, I know that I am too.*

"Sorry," I squeaked quietly. I closed my eyes, thinking of last night. My pinkie began to twitch. I sighed to myself and shoved my hand into my pocket, trying to keep my twitching at bay while I was daydreaming of last night.

I remembered slowly opening my eyes from my nap last night, feeling Cole's warm arms around me. I gently touched his arm and looked up at him. He gave me a soft look before he pulled away and apologized to me.

"You just seemed to be having a nightmare. I only wanted to comfort you," he said. He started to stand up and walk away, but I stopped him. I took his hand and gave him a little smile.

"Thanks," I whispered with a smile. We stared into each other's eyes. I couldn't help but blush and look away.

Cole gently grabbed my chin and pulled me toward him. We leaned into one another, embracing as we kissed one another. I gingerly grabbed his cheek as he pulled me closer. My hand gently moved from his cheek to the back of his head.

After a few more moments, we pulled away. We both blushed and turned away from one another, surprised at ourselves.

Cole cleared his throat, suddenly becoming distant. "Sorry. Excuse me." He got up and walked away before I could stop him.

I cleared my throat, coming out of my daydream as I swallowed my tears. He helped me unload my suitcase.

"Have a safe journey back," he said.

"Thanks," I said, trying not to choke. I looked down toward the cement before looking back up. "Cole . . . "

"Yeah?"

"I love you. I know if we start a relationship it probably wouldn't work out the way we'd want it to, but . . . I'm willing to be yours." I said. More tears came to my eyes.

Cole's eyes glossed over with his own tears. He examined me as I held onto my suitcase tightly. My knuckles began to go white.

"I love you too, Crystal Ann." he said.

He brought me into a hug, holding me tight. "I can't let you go anymore. If we really love each other, why would you have to go? Can't you stay?"

I held him tightly as I gave a sad chuckle. "I have a life back in New York. I have a family. I can't just drop everything and leave. It would disappoint a lot of people if I didn't come back. I have to write my article. I have to be able to say goodbye to my family. What would that make me if I really just dropped everything to stay here?"

We took a step away from each other as we gazed into each other's eyes. I put my hand on his shoulder as I fell into his chest once more. I caressed his cheek as I looked up at him. He held me around my waist. My heart pounded. I could feel his was pounding too. My pinkie felt like it was on fire, but I knew I could ignore it for now.

"I can't deny that," he whispered. A tear fell from his eyes. I gently wiped it away as I ruffled the back of his short hair.

"We can make a deal with each other. How about, once everything has cleared up. . . Maybe, I can return?" I asked.

Cole couldn't help but smile. "I would like that very much. But, I can't live a day without you. How—"

I cut him off as I said, "We'll exchange every way we can keep in contact with each other. Phone numbers, emails, and anything else you can think of to help us stay in contact. I will always make the effort if you will too."

He gave a nod as we exchanged phones and added each other on everything we could think of.

An announcement came over the speakers calling my flight. We both looked up, listening to the message before looking back at one another. We smiled at each other as we leaned in and kissed once more.

"Goodbye for now, Mr. Cole Dakota." I said.

"Goodbye for now, my dearest Crystal Ann Alston." he spoke quietly.

As we looked at each other in the moment, I saw the look in his eyes that told me I'd have to wait for a while. I drew in a deep breath, trying to be brave. I turned away. As I began to walk, I felt a small tug on my hand. I looked down and saw a glimmering red thread. I followed the thread back to Cole's hand. I smiled and gave one last wave before I walked inside the airport by myself. I was escorted through the airport and put on his plane back to NYC.

Chapter Sixteen

My Time with Cole Dakota
By: Crystal Ann Alston

I had the opportunity to spend a couple of weeks shadowing Cole Dakota to see what it would be like to be a movie star. Let me tell you, it is not easy. In addition to shadowing him, I also had the pleasure of asking more about his past and the events that led up to him being the movie star that he is today.

First, though, I will talk about what it's like being a star before going into more details about Mr. Dakota. Although, on the screen, it may seem that being an actor is easy, shadowing Cole these past few weeks has definitely not been easy. It's been early morning after early morning before running around until I felt like my legs were about to fall off. Not only that, but sometimes, if the director called for it, he had to do the same scene over and over again. Sometimes so many times that even a professional could be brought to tears by the stress of doing the same thing over and over again. It's also hard to think what effect this work has on the mind.

I can't say what movie Cole Dakota was in the middle of filming (as I have been sworn to secrecy), but being on set was definitely a treat. I had the chance to talk to his makeup artists who have been in their business for nearly twelve years. If you don't know who makes Cole look like a star for the silver screen, their names are Ava and Lucy Green. They're sisters and have been in this business long enough to not just be the makeup artists for Cole Dakota, but for several other actors as well. So, if you think that your favorite star is looking especially good on the screen, you could thank the Green sisters. Do make sure to watch for their names in the credits. That's why the credits are there.

Watching Cole Dakota in the makeup chair, even though the Green sisters know and are great at their craft, did look like torture. It didn't seem pleasant whatsoever. So, if you have a fear of other people painting your face, I will say that acting probably isn't for you.

One thing that is definitely hard about acting is someone always telling you that you could do better, even when you're doing the best you can. Sometimes Mr. Dakota, or another actor/actress would forget a line or act completely different from what the director wanted. Joe Bronson, the director of this film, would act out exactly what he wanted from the actors or even talk to them face to face. However, most of the time, to save time, he'd yell at them, giving them vague cues to follow. Being yelled at for doing something that was vague in the first place would be frustrating.

I am not saying being a movie star is all hard and awful. There is definitely some fun on set. Sometimes, during intense scenes, it's hard not to smile when actors have to stare at each other for hours on end. It becomes harder to control yourself and keep yourself from laughing after the first time someone slips up and laughs during what is supposed to be an epic moment.

One thing I will applaud actors on is kissing people without ever developing feelings for them. I'm not sure if I could kiss them without liking them first. It is especially difficult to make it look passionate enough for us, the viewers. I'm not sure how some stars' wives or husbands do it. Kissing others, definitely good-looking people, all day every day? I might get a little jealous if I were in their shoes.

The method of acting that I witnessed was a treat. Mr. Dakota tries to be serious most of the time, being dedicated to his craft for his fans, but he can't help but crack up sometimes. I think his hardest scenes to stay calm in were the ones where it was supposed to be romantic, staring into an actress's eyes. I'm not sure I could blame him for laughing. Especially if he were in love with someone else or the actress he was filming with was a good friend.

Now as I promised, I'll share the story of how Mr. Cole Dakota came to be the star he is today. It all started when he was four years old. He had watched all the movies his family owned at least ten times each month. He followed the acting he saw on television. When his parents, soon to be only his father, as his mother passed away when he was seven, wouldn't let him watch the same movie over and over again, he'd just watch the television, mimicking those actors.

When he was five, his parents felt comfortable enough to let him act in the city play. It was free except for providing costumes. Mr. Dakota found his passion for acting. When he was younger, he always played the small parts, like a child running around the grown adults on the stage for the play. Cole really appreciates his dad for putting up with him wanting to do these things, as it couldn't have been easy for him to listen to him blurting out his lines in the car, or singing whenever they did musicals, but he kept at it.

When he went to middle school and high school, all he ever did was perform in their plays. He also continued to act in the city plays. It was definitely his passion. He did say that he was bullied a little bit by a better actor in his class, but his drama teacher in high school inspired him to keep going. The drama teacher, during one of his performances where he was the star of the show, actually called a recruiting officer to see if he could be recruited for Broadway or a movie.

The recruiter liked Cole Dakota so much that he asked the drama teacher to film his performances. He sent them to directors and executives to get his name out there—to get him into Hollywood.

It didn't take long for people to see how talented he was, and they were twice as fast to reach out to his dad, and now a stepmother as well, and to give them the opportunity to let their son shine on the silver screen. His parents almost didn't accept at first, but wanted to talk to Mr. Dakota, who seized the opportunity and became what he is today. His parents made sure he finished his schooling first and continued his education at least part-time in college.

His first movie was a remake of the old classic, Gone With the Wind. He was only seventeen at the time. He played a background role, but it helped him get his start.

Keeping the promise he made to his parents, he went to school part-time, and at some points, when there were no projects for him to do, he went full-time. He got his degree in environmental science with a minor in theater. He told me he is a lot smarter than he looks. I was told that his IQ score was at least 163.

Cole Dakota wanted me to write that he really appreciates all the things that have happened in his life. He told me that he was fortunate to be in his line of work, and he has his fans and those directors and recruiters that helped get him started to thank for his success. He always gives them credit whenever he's received an award. By the way, Cole Dakota has received ten awards within the last three years of his career.

I did ask Cole Dakota if he donated some of his money to charity, to which he told me that when all his bills are paid and he has some money in savings and some spent on himself, he gives the rest to the needy. I find that amazing.

In closing, Cole Dakota believes that his life was an easy one. Looking at it from the outside in, I believe he was being humble. He definitely deserves the world for what he's been through and for what he does for others. If you're a fan of Cole Dakota, thanks for being so. That's from Cole himself. And if you're not a fan of his, maybe it's time you should be.

Chapter Seventeen

I stared into my cup of iced tea. I looked around the busy Starbucks. My article was published about Cole; it was a big hit. I received my money and was living happily, at least as best I could. It had been a few months since I had seen Cole, but I knew he'd come for me. He'd come for me because of that story. The story of The Red Thread of Destiny.

My best memory of our time together was when he told me about that legend. My life seemed to make a lot more sense after he told me. I stared out the window, the glass playing what had happened between us when he told me that story.

We were in New York, on the ferry traveling from Liberty Island back to New York.

"You keep mentioning this 'red thread of fate' or something." I said.

"It's a story from Asia." Cole said.

"All right. Tell me about it."

"There is a story of this young couple. Their villages are at war. They met once atop a hill. It was late into the spring and another battle between the rivaling villages

was about to break out. They looked at each other for only a moment, until a red thread appeared on their pinkies. They looked at each other with surprise. They ran away from one another for some time. They seemed to either be scared of each other or too shy.

"The woman helped in her fields, gathering seeds from the mountaintop where she had met the boy, but the boy was fighting in the war during the warmer months. He was fighting for his village.

"The next spring they met once again. Their threads pulling them together this time, making them put aside their cautions. They began to talk to one another about the war and how it should end. They soon began to meet every day, slowly falling in love with one another.

"They went to their parents and proposed how they could end this war, even though the girl's father was not the head of their village. The girl's father then went to the village leader and told him about this plan. The man thought the father was crazy and sent him away.

"But the boy's father believed him, as he was their village's head, and brought a white flag over to the other village. He asked to speak with the head of the village as he wanted to make peace. Soon, after they talked, they saw that their differences could not be met. The boy's father forbid he see the woman, but that didn't stop them."

"How rude," I interrupted. "That should've definitely stopped the feud!"

Cole laughed as he had continued. "One day, the young couple agreed they would kill each other on the battlefield to stop this senseless war—and that's what they did."

"Wait!" I interrupted again. "Is that the Japanese version of Romeo and Juliet?"

Cole shook his head. "This one came first if I remember right. Now let me finish."

"Sorry."

"They wouldn't let the war between their villages keep them apart any longer. Their red thread kept them together in the life after, and they lived happily there. They were happy in death. The two villages stopped feuding for the loss of two beautiful lovers."

"How star-crossed."

"I just don't want us to end up that way," Cole said.

"You keep that up, and we're going to end up together," I snorted, trying to hide my feelings.

"Well, hopefully it'll end up that way."

I smiled to myself, thinking of that fond memory. Cole had been overseas on location for the past few months. Keeping in contact had been hard, but well worth it.

I felt my pinkie twitch slightly as I saw something red sparkle from the corner of my eye. I shook my head to myself, trying to ignore that feeling as I heard my name from an all too familiar voice. I stood up from my seat and turned around to see him.

"It's hard to find you in this big city," Cole said.

"I'd hope you let your string guide you," I teased.

He got down onto his knee. "Marry me?" he asked.

"I've been waiting for you for so long, Cole. Yes." I wrapped my arms around him as I knelt down in front of him, giving him a big kiss as people around us began to clap.